WALKING IN ALEXA'S SHOES

A BOOK OF RHYME,
BACK IN TIME ...

ROCHELLE ALEXANDRA

WALKING
IN ALEXA'S
SHOES

A BOOK OF RHYME,
BACK IN TIME ...

"You should write it my darling,
if it's something you'd want to do.
So the world knows what happened,
to both Polish Gentile and Jew."

~ Alexa ~

CONTENTS

PREFACE

I was truly blessed to have one of the most amazing women as my grandmother. I adored Alexa and loved spending time together chatting over cups of tea when I'd visit her in Poland with my mother during summer vacations as a child.

I knew she had been taken to Germany with her mother to work when she was a child, but that was all I knew. It wasn't until I spent seven weeks with my grandmother back in November 2002, when she shared her wartime experiences and harrowing life story with me.

I promised my grandmother I'd write her story into a novel one day, reimagined and told my way. Thankfully, I was able to keep that promise and published my debut historical novel *IN ALEXA'S SHOES* back in June of 2019. Sadly, Alexa passed away five weeks before it was released. I'm delighted by the many reader's responses, reviews, recommendations and #1 bestseller badges on Amazon internationally so far, as would have been my Babcia.

With the sincere hope of educating and reaching many teens and young readers, I was inspired to write a version of Alexa's story in rhyme form. I always had a love for poetry as a child, and its therapeutic value. I hope others will be inspired to create their own poems and rhymes relating to the tough times they may be going through in their own lives, as a means of enduring hardships, with the hope of triumphing over them.

Hate is a poison. Love is the answer!
We must never forget!

~ 1 ~

SCHOOL'S OUT

Hitler invaded Poland,
on September 1ˢᵗ, 1939.
When life as Polish people knew it,
was heinously changed for all time.

Alexa sat by the classroom window,
gazing out at the trees.
Transfixed by the dance of autumn,
as she watched the falling leaves.

Reds, yellows, coppers, and rusts,
tapestries of color on display.
In her head she heard the violins,
of Vivaldi's 'Four Seasons' play.

Daydreaming about the new pair of shoes,
her mother had promised to buy.
An unusual sight came into view,
from the corner of her eye.

Men in ragged clothing,
carried shovels into the woods.
Marched at gunpoint by Nazi soldiers,
their outcome didn't look good.

The school bell rang unusually early,
the class made its way outside.
Nazi trucks were parked at the gate,
there was nowhere to run or hide.

Ordered to line up in pairs,
Alexa took Helena's hand.
They marched on the road together,
as fast as their feet could land.

Alexa said her prayer to herself,
and recited Psalm 91.
It gave her a sense of protection,
so she wasn't afraid of their guns.

Teachers marched with the students,
who were still under their care.
Everyone obeyed orders,
avoiding the soldiers' glare.

A silent longing for their mothers,
expressed on each child's face.
Which became their motivation,
marching to the soldiers' pace.

2

As they walked along the roadway,
and the village came into view.
The soldiers and their barking Alsatians,
pulled off from the road in twos.

Light chatter began among the children,
as the soldiers started to retract.
She told Helena she could try her new shoes,
on Monday, when school was back.

As Alexa's house got closer,
her best friend said goodbye.
She blew a kiss in the wind,
and offered it up to the sky.

After waving farewell to Helena,
she ran home and closed the front door.
Alexa fell into her mother's arms,
and wasn't afraid anymore.

Her mother Sophia became anxious,
seeing her daughter so distraught.
Alexa began explaining the nightmare,
in which she had just been caught.

Sophia hugged her thirteen-year-old,
holding her tightly in her arms.
"It's okay my darling, you're safe now.
I won't let you come to harm."

She began boiling some water,
making Alexa a hot cup of tea.
She added some sliced lemon,
and a spoonful of sweet honey.

They agreed it best not to tell Asha,
as it would only cause her distress.
She was very much the worrying type,
who would overthink and obsess.

Alexa's younger sister Asha,
was only eight years old.
And was already showing symptoms,
of a slight flu or cold.

She hadn't left the house that day,
a sore throat developed through the night.
Her mother insisted she stay in bed,
and checked to make sure she was all right.

Her mother kept her home from school,
where she lay in bed with a fever.
Playing with her mother's wedding rings,
before the next day they'd both leave her.

Sophia went next door to Magda,
her friend and German neighbor.
To ask if she could look after Asha,
as a one-off kind of favor.

Magda said she was available,
and asked Sophia what time.
"We'll leave early in the morning,
can you come to my house for nine?"

Sophia returned to her girls,
who were reading together in bed.
She recited Psalm 91,
then kissed each on their forehead.

Sophia retrieved the glass jar,
where she'd hidden saved money away.
Then counted out on the table,
how much she needed for the next day.

Sophia lived alone with her two daughters,
since the death of her husband and mum.
Both had been great role models to the girls,
before their life course was done.

Alexander, her husband, a successful artist,
tried to teach Alexa all he knew.
With a heightened sense of urgency,
knowing his days left on earth were few.

Sarah, her widowed mother,
came to live with them at their home.
Helping to raise her granddaughters,
so Sophia wasn't alone.

She'd been such a positive influence,
sharing her belief in God above.
She adored both of her grandchildren,
and showered them with love.

She taught them Psalm 91,
helping them learn a rhyme from school.
The girls took turns reciting it,
as their morning and night-time ritual.

Sadly, Sarah died suddenly,
only two years before.
But her memory lived on,
in their hearts forever more.

Saturday morning arrived,
and Alexa dressed in dark blue.
Wearing a navy skirt and cardigan,
to match her new blue shoes.

They both kissed Asha goodbye,
saying they wouldn't be away long.
Magda knocked on their door at nine,
and within minutes, they were both gone.

Psalm 91

~ 2 ~

NEW SHOES

Alexa left home with her mother,
and walked toward the town square.
With a vibrant spring in her step,
and a bounce in her long blonde hair.

She saw Karolina with her brother,
through the window of the butcher's shop.
She quickly waved to them both,
but didn't have time to stop.

Finally, she arrived at the store,
where she'd buy her lovely new shoes.
She really liked the red Patent ones,
but she knew she'd choose the blues.

A shiny brass bell rang above them,
as they stepped inside the door.
She sat her coat on a nearby chair,
kicking her old shoes to the floor.

A Polish woman in her late fifties,
neatly dressed, hair tied up in a bun.
Showed them the shoes she had on display,
and asked if they'd like to try some.

Sophia pointed to a blue pair of shoes,
she wanted her daughter to try.
The obliging shopkeeper soon returned,
with a pair she guessed was her size.

Sophia asked for a bigger pair,
giving Alexa more room to grow.
The woman brought size thirties,
and Alexa slipped in her toes.

Admiring the shoes in a long mirror,
the silver buckles shone in the light.
Alexa walked on the wooden floor,
the small heel gave her more height.

"How do they feel my darling?
are they comfortable on your feet?"
"Oh yes Mamma, I love them."
"Then you can have them, my sweet."

Alexa looked back in the mirror,
but the reflection behind her had changed.
She saw locals running in the town square,
looking panicked and deranged.

A roll of thunder rumbled outside,
taking the females by surprise.
They saw the horrific nightmare unfold,
before their very eyes.

Their faces were panic-stricken,
there was nowhere for them to hide.
The brass bell rang a warning sound,
as Nazi soldiers burst inside.

They were ordered out onto the street,
and lined up with all the others.
Alexa spotted Karolina,
holding the hand of her little brother.

The shopkeeper became irate,
protesting there'd been a mistake.
"I'm an honest, hardworking Polish woman.
Let me go, for God's sake!"

Sophia squeezed Alexa's hand tightly,
telling her to look at her shoes and pray.
While the Nazi officer in charge,
aimed his attention the shopkeeper's way.

"Honest and hardworking,
that's a lie right there."
Then he reached for his side pistol,
and raised it to the air.

"I hope you lazy Poles,
work harder than the filthy Jews."
The woman became hysterical,
and was shaking in her shoes.

Taking aim he pulled the trigger,
and the woman fell to the ground.
As her head hit the cobbles,
it made a loud cracking sound.

"Let that be a warning to you all,
to follow the orders I give!
Shut up and do as you are told,
especially if you want to live."

The locals were rounded up by age,
and loaded onto five trucks.
Separated from their mothers,
the kinder were out of luck.

Children cried out and mothers screamed,
desperately searching for each other.
Karolina huddled close with Alexa,
no longer with her little brother.

Alexa tightly closed her eyes,
and began to recite her prayer.
Hoping God would hear her,
and keep them in His care.

"Alexa, Alexa!"
Sophia screamed out her name.
"Mamma! Mamma!" She yelled back,
but her voice called out in vain.

10

Herded into dirty cattle wagons,
at the Lublin train station.
The terrified locals had no idea,
of their final destination.

Crammed in with a hundred strangers,
sat on the carriage's filthy floor.
There were no windows to escape through,
Nazi soldiers firmly bolted the door.

There wasn't any food or drink,
for the prisoners to consume.
Nor any privacy to use the bucket,
substituted as a bathroom.

The stench was absolutely putrid,
and many people became ill.
In bouts of uncontrollable gagging,
each time the waste bucket would spill.

There were small holes in the wagon's walls,
where bitter cold winds blew through.
Alexa and Karolina huddled close together,
sharing some warmth between the two.

Alexa recited Psalm 91,
she needed God's help more than ever.
But despite the hopeless situation,
she never doubted He would deliver.

After days of the nightmare journey,
the transportation finally stopped.
As the doors were forcefully flung open,
to the ground the prisoners dropped.

Frantically searching around them,
Alexa found her mother on the tracks.
While Nazi soldiers screamed and yelled,
striking batons on the prisoner's backs.

Desperate people scanned the scene,
for their young children and elderlies.
Not knowing they'd already gone,
to sleep in the forest with the trees.

Ferocious, hungry, wild, barking dogs,
snapped and snarled as they stood on guard.
While soldiers removed their valuables,
demanding their identity cards.

Most prisoners were sent to the left,
others, to a line on the right.
The helpless souls on the wrong side,
disappeared completely from sight.

By name, age, religion, and gender,
the right were ordered into huts.
They frantically ran inside,
while being struck by rifle butts.

Alexa's mother searched the barracks,
for a vacant bunk they could share.
She cuddled in close to her daughter,
stroking her soft, long, blonde hair.

The wooden bunks were packed with women,
maybe five or six deep.
But with no blankets, mattresses, or pillows,
it was near impossible to sleep.

Early morning roll call began,
and the women stood to attention.
Each of their names were yelled out,
not one avoided a mention.

A second roll call was ordered,
everyone quickly stepped back into line.
But little did Alexa know,
she'd see her mother for the last time.

A female Kapo shouted orders,
and with her baton struck Alexa's hand.
Then violently struck her mother's head,
who collapsed in a heap on the sand.

Separated from her injured mother,
Alexa was dragged to a waiting truck.
Then piled inside with a group of teens,
she immediately prayed for some luck.

13

Psalm 91 was her go-to prayer,
she recited it day and night.
Whenever consumed by darkness,
it brought her hope and light.

~ 3 ~

SLAVING FOR THE ENEMY

The truck stopped outside of a building,
which was draped in Nazi flags.
The teenagers stood in a line-up,
dressed in their worn and tattered rags.

Next, there was a selection made,
and the group was split into two.
Alexa was led inside the building,
while others disappeared from view.

It suddenly occurred to her,
those selected all looked the same.
With their blue eyes and blonde hair,
all that was missing, was a German name.

They were given some milk and a slice of bread,
then their faces and hands were cleaned.
Once presentable they were marched to a room,
where they waited to be screened.

Ten of the youths were again lined up,
and waited to learn their fate.
Then SS Officers and their wives,
chose a slave to drive out the gate.

One wife pointed to Alexa's neck,
spotting the cross hanging from her chain.
She asked if the girl was Catholic,
to which Alexa nodded yes, again.

With no choice in the matter,
she was selected by Frau and Herr Klauss.
But little did she know she'd become a slave,
at their German farmhouse.

Bundled into the back of his car,
Herr Klauss drove her to his farm.
Alexa slept the whole way there,
with her head resting on her arm.

"Wake up Alexa, we are home."
Were the words she heard from Herr Klauss.
But as she stepped out of the vehicle,
she clearly wasn't at her own house.

In the kitchen a Polish-speaking soldier,
read a list of her demanding chores.
She'd slave each day until eleven at night,
beginning her work in the morning at four.

She'd work seven days and for all that labor,
she wouldn't receive a wage.
The soldier continued reading the list,
flipping over to the fourth page.

Alexa was deflated,
and could hardly stand on her feet.
Once the soldier finished reading,
he pointed to some food she could eat.

"Bring the sandwich and cup of milk,
and follow me upstairs."
Alexa did as she was told,
and silently recited her prayers.

Taken to a dark, filthy, attic room,
and locked inside all alone.
Alexa couldn't help but wonder,
if she'd ever make it back home.

Her thoughts ran back to her sister,
whom they'd left with the next-door neighbor.
She'd looked after Asha while they shopped,
before they were taken as slave labor.

Where was she now, and how would she cope?
Alexa made her petitions known to God.
Keeping the hope she'd find her again,
and be freed from her captor's rod.

Alexa was exhausted,
and could no longer hold up her head.
She cried herself to sleep,
on the old, rusty, metal bed.

Early the next morning,
a key turned in the door's metal lock.
A German woman shouted out,
"Time for work! It's four o'clock."

Her new blue shoes were taken from her,
and replaced by large wooden clogs.
While kept under the watchful eye,
of Herr Klauss's barking dogs.

To cook, clean, and care for their kids,
her chores never seemed to end.
She also worked the farmland,
for hours on her knees she'd bend.

Alexa toiled from morning till night,
and daily she'd recite her prayer.
Always with the assured expectation,
she'd rest in God's protective care.

Seasons changed and four years went by,
while Alexa slaved for the Klausses.
Just as many other children were forced,
to work for German farmhouses.

As hard as it was, she did a good job,
always trying to do her best.
No matter the challenge or difficulty,
she viewed it all as a test.

In time the Klausses rewarded her efforts,
giving her a slightly better room.
It even had a skylight window,
from which she could see the moon.

She was allowed to sit at their table,
when the holidays would come.
Even though she'd prepared all the food,
they invited her to eat some.

She was gifted a Bible in German,
similar to the one she'd read as a child.
It was what she'd secretly prayed for.
"Thank you kindly," Alexa smiled.

She wasn't allowed to speak Polish,
since the first day she'd arrived at the farm.
But always prayed in her mother tongue,
when silently reciting the Psalm.

She slaved until almost midnight,
before her workday came to an end.
Bloomshen, a sympathetic dairy cow,
became her confidant and friend.

She could speak to it in Polish,
and it seemed to understand.
As she shared her thoughts and feelings,
from its eye, a tear would land.

She milked a total of twelve cows,
two times every day.
She tended to the horses,
refreshing their water and hay.

There were chickens and pigs to feed,
and eggs to gather from the barn.
She learned her tasks very quickly,
for someone who'd never been on a farm.

The children grew quite fond of Alexa,
and liked being under her care.
They actually all looked related,
with their blue eyes and Aryan blonde hair.

Her father had taught her his talent for art,
from a very early age.
Alexa could effortlessly draw sketches,
bringing them to life on a blank page.

Fredrick was Herr Klauss's cousin,
he served as the local Catholic Priest.
He said the girl was technically an orphan,
with both her parents now gone, or deceased.

So, the Klausses had a duty of care,
to see that she came to no real harm.
Which must have excluded the forced labor,
she was expected to work on their farm.

~ 4 ~

PARTY SHOES

The war raged on across Europe,
with soldiers, killings, and bombs.
Jews were sent to prison camps,
who'd actually done nothing wrong.

Hitler's wicked, sadistic regime,
spread terror across many lands.
His army of vicious soldiers,
had innocent blood on their hands.

Men, women, children, and babies,
were all forced against their will.
To slave in concentration camps,
or become a soldier's kill.

Their homes, possessions, and families,
away from them were torn.
Separated from each other,
for the rest of their lives, they'd mourn.

Alexa continued to give her best,
in each task she was forced to do.
She continued reciting Psalm 91,
praying her wish would one day come true.

That her forced labor would come to an end,
and she'd return to those who missed her.
That she'd finally be reunited,
with her mother and younger sister.

Herr Klauss arranged to throw a party,
inviting soldiers and some local girls.
Who'd twirl them on the dance floor,
in a mix of spins and waltzing whirls.

Alexa was also invited,
after all the preparations were complete.
She was given a pretty blue dress to wear,
and a pair of normal shoes for her feet.

When she opened the bag and looked inside,
her heart skipped a beat.
She'd been given back her new blue shoes,
which only just, still fit her feet.

Two other local slave girls,
whom Alexa knew were there.
They too had cleaned up nicely,
letting down their long blonde hair.

A problem arose when Alexa arrived,
the soldiers became visibly distracted.
There was no denying her natural beauty,
to which the males were clearly attracted.

They made their interest known,
taking Alexa to the dance floor.
But her friends became overly jealous,
as she was forced to dance some more.

Once the music had ended,
Alexa left the party making an excuse.
Her friendship with the girls, was more important,
that, she didn't want to lose.

Once the party was over,
Alexa had the clean-up job to do.
She took off the pretty party dress,
and gave back her new blue shoes.

Herr Klauss's home office was private,
he kept it under lock and key.
It was a rule strictly adhered to,
no one entered it, but he.

Alexa asked no questions,
she had quickly learned her place.
And was able to hide her emotions,
disguising the expressions on her face.

She developed a special skill set,
of masking how she really felt.
So no one knew her true feelings,
on the cards she was actually dealt.

23

One day the Klausses trusted Alexa,
to collect some bespoke new shoes.
She'd cross the border wearing a 'P',
not a 'yellow star' like the Jews.

It could have been her one chance to escape,
to make a run for it on her own.
But she knew she would never survive,
walking to Poland, on foot alone.

She crossed a white bridge in her wooden clogs,
making her way to the shoemaker's store.
But the woman immediately became concerned,
when Alexa walked through the door.

She inquired as to who she was,
and what she was doing there.
She seemed genuinely interested,
showing real concern and care.

When she said she slaved for the Klausses,
Alice Klein refused to let her depart.
Showing the kindness of a stranger,
with real empathy from her heart.

"How dare they," she said,
"I can help make your getaway.
I have a cousin living in Belgium,
where I'm sure she'd let you stay."

She locked up the shop, took Alexa to her home,
and made her something to eat.
Where she could relax and feel free for a while,
removing the clogs from her aching feet.

She had a hot bath, was given clean clothes,
then shown to a warm, comfortable bed.
But was unable to fully relax,
knowing Herr Klauss would be seething bright red.

He drove to the Kleins' house at sunrise,
insisting Alexa come straight out.
His temper was boiling over,
as he yelled his demands loudly out.

Mr Klein knew Herr Klauss,
they campaigned on the political stage.
Over coffee they discussed Alexa's future,
while Herr Klauss calmed down his rage.

An agreement was reached Alexa would return,
to work for Frau and Herr Klauss.
They decided she'd have Sunday afternoons off,
as a guest at the Kleins' house.

Every Sunday she'd walk for an hour,
across the border to her little retreat.
The Kleins' adored Alexa,
and made new shoes for her feet.

She was always warmly welcomed,
and made to feel at home.
It gave her extra endurance,
for the times when she slaved alone.

Her hours spent in Luxembourg,
with Mr and Mrs Klein.
Were amongst the happiest days,
Alexa spent during wartime.

~ 5 ~

THE OFFICE ESCAPE

During December of 1944,
the war across Europe raged on.
With many night-time bombing raids,
leaving devastating casualties at dawn.

It was a severe Baltic winter,
which made living conditions hard.
For both soldiers and civilians,
and prisoners locked behind bars.

One night Herr Klauss asked Alexa,
to step into his private office.
Since it had never happened before,
Alexa was naturally cautious.

"We are giving you back your freedom,
here's a ticket for a first-class train."
Alexa couldn't believe her ears,
and asked Herr Klauss to say it again.

Alexa was in disbelief,
at the words she'd heard him say.
Then she innocently blurted out,
"But I do not know the way."

Frau Klauss seemed surprised,
hearing Alexa's honest reply.
She appeared overwhelmed,
as if she was about to cry.

"We got you a ticket to make your escape,
and begin your journey back home.
Edgar will drive you to the station,
but you'll make the rest of the journey alone."

"I've written down the directions,
of where you have to go.
There's a convent in Kreuzberg,
with a nun there whom I know."

"Once you leave the train carriage,
you'll walk through a forest for a while.
Then you'll pass a small village,
and the convent is less than a mile."

Alexa was utterly elated,
her excitement hard to contain.
But she masked her inner feelings,
and hid them once again.

"You'll leave here tomorrow at noon,
for the one o'clock train to Berlin.
18A in the first-class carriage,
that's the seat you'll be sitting in."

"I got you some forged German papers,
we'll give you money before you leave.
You'll not wear the letter 'P' anymore,
sewn onto your jacket sleeve."

Alexa kindly thanked Herr Klauss,
for helping her get back home.
She also thanked her God above,
in her room, when she was alone.

She was given a small black suitcase,
in which to pack her few belongings.
Some clothes, her Bible, a hair clip, and comb,
and one of her favorite drawings.

She also packed her old blue shoes,
although they no longer fit her feet.
She wanted to show her mother,
she'd kept them from that day in the street.

She memorized the list of directions,
given to her by Herr Klauss.
He'd instructed her to destroy them,
before departing from his house.

Her final night in the Klausses home,
was surreal in so many ways.
She reflected on her stolen youth,
working as an unpaid slave.

On all the things taken from her,
and all the things she had lost.
On all the things she'd missed out on,
and the relationships war had cost.

But then she thought of the elation,
once her family was reunited.
She kept that her main focus,
in her mind's-eye, she delighted.

Choosing to dwell on the positives,
and the new road which lay ahead.
She pulled the blankets under her chin,
for the last night in her prisoner's bed.

She began to say her prayer,
reciting Psalm 91.
Thanking God for keeping her safe,
and away from the soldier's gun.

Alexa's last day as an unpaid slave,
arrived with the rising sun.
She made sure all of her chores,
were completed and perfectly done.

Instructed not to tell the children,
she'd be leaving the house that day.
It wasn't how she wanted it,
but she didn't have any say.

She'd grown attached to the children,
caring for them for four years.
As she waved them off to school,
her eyes filled up with tears.

Cousin Edgar arrived at the farm,
to drive Alexa in Herr Klauss's car.
"It won't take very long," he said,
the train station isn't very far.

Frau Klauss extended more kindness,
giving her shoes, a scarf, and warm coat.
Herr Klauss gave her some German marks,
for the journey, to keep afloat.

He thanked Alexa for all the work,
she had done while on his farm.
Then he ripped the 'P' off her sleeve,
removing the Polish badge from her arm.

Alexa sat in the car's front seat,
taking one final look back at the place.
She was filled with mixed emotions,
but never expressed them on her face.

Fredrick started the engine,
steering the car down the tree-lined drive.
The Klausses waved goodbye and said,
"Let's pray she makes it home alive."

He stopped the car underneath a bridge.
as they neared the railway station.
Alexa walked to the platform herself,
taking each step without hesitation.

An elderly couple sat on a bench,
waiting for the Berlin train.
The old man looked up at the clock,
then stared back down the tracks again.

Alexa thought of the parallel,
of the two separate steel tracks.
Although separated in front of her,
in the distance they seemed to join back.

She thought how the first train journey,
with her mother had torn them apart.
But this was her return journey,
hopefully soon, their reunion could start.

A whistle blew off in the distance,
and the steel rails began to vibrate.
As the passenger train came into view,
the man seemed relieved it wasn't late.

~ 6 ~

A FIRST-CLASS TICKET

Alexa approached the first-class carriage,
and opened up the door.
But as she stepped inside the train,
her heart sank to the floor.

Never could she have imagined,
the scene which lay before her eyes.
She quickly drew from her skill set,
keeping her true emotions disguised.

The compartment was full of SS,
Nazi soldiers filled every seat.
Alexa had no time to react,
she had to think fast on her feet.

She walked along the aisle full of men,
trying to locate her reserved seat.
Eventually, she found one marked A18,
and placed her suitcase by her feet.

Every male was distracted by her,
making her uncomfortable with their stare.
But she didn't show a reaction,
instead she smiled and flicked her hair.

She reached for her Bible,
and thumbed through its pages.
Time sped by on the journey,
she'd been reading for ages.

When she looked up from her book,
she was no longer in the soldier's view.
So she took the opportunity,
to visit the onboard loo.

She stepped inside and locked the door,
relieved to finally be on her own.
She washed her face, looked in the mirror,
then said, "Mamma, I'm coming home."

Not wanting to draw attention,
by staying in the toilet too long.
She straightened up her clothes,
wore a brave face and walked on.

The soldiers in the compartment,
were smoking and drinking schnapps.
Some gambled in card games,
while others browsed their maps.

Some were cleaning their rifles,
loading them with ammunition.
Alexa once again found herself,
in a most difficult position.

Allied troops landed in Germany,
and the war was nearing its end.
But Hitler wouldn't surrender the Fatherland,
his soldiers fought hard to defend.

Alexa had to be careful,
that her cover wasn't blown.
She knew she'd most likely be shot,
if her true identity was known.

She now spoke fluent German,
and could pass for one of them.
But she despised the Nazi regime,
their vile actions she condemned.

A conductor appeared in the compartment,
and seemed surprised by Alexa being there.
He demanded to see her ticket,
to make sure she'd paid the correct fare.

She handed over her ticket,
which the conductor looked at up close.
Then he began shouting irately,
as if someone had stood on his toes.

"This isn't a first-class ticket,
you shouldn't be sitting here.
You'll have to leave this carriage,
and sit somewhere in the rear."

Alexa was embarrassed,
she didn't know what to do.
Then suddenly an officer stood up and said,
"I'll pay the rest of the ticket for you."

He asked the conductor how much it cost,
to give her ticket an upgrade.
He made a new one valid for first class,
which the stranger happily paid.

Alexa was very grateful,
but didn't quite know what to say.
She thanked the officer in German,
who in return, wished her a good day.

Alexa watched the snow fall outside,
through the window of the train.
She dreaded the next part of her journey,
in frozen temperatures and harsh terrain.

The train approached the Potsdam crossing,
where she'd been instructed to alight.
She wasn't wearing a watch,
but figured it must be seven at night.

As she stood up from her seat,
making her way to the carriage door.
A soldier ordered her to stop,
and again, her heart hit the floor.

She slowly turned around,
to face the direction of the man.
"Frauline, you forgot your glove!"
He said, holding it up in his hand.

Alexa breathed a sigh of relief,
taking her glove from his hand.
Jumping down from the train's steps,
the soft snow cushioned her land.

She had a really bad feeling,
as the soldiers watched her walk away.
They followed her from open windows,
but not a word did they say.

She imagined the soldiers behind her,
taking aim with their guns at her head.
Alexa defiantly decided,
that's not how she wanted to end up dead.

She turned around to face them,
as the train began to move on.
And within less than a minute,
the train was completely gone.

Alexa had given a flawless performance,
and had the soldiers completely misled.
It wasn't so much she had lied to them,
but rather, they had totally misread.

She began to recite her Psalm,
praying it up to God in heaven.
Thanking him for the protection,
she believed that He had given.

~ 7 ~

A WALK IN THE FOREST

Alexa left the railroad tracks,
walking towards a main street.
Then headed into the forest.
crunching crisp snow under her feet.

Herr Klauss had told Alexa,
to walk a distance in through the trees.
Since Nazi trucks were on the move,
so she'd be hidden by the leaves.

She stepped into her pajamas,
and tucked them into her socks.
Then wrapped the scarf around her head,
to the sound of a howling fox.

As she recited Psalm 91,
it asked for protection from snakes and bears.
Alexa hadn't stopped to think,
of the wild animals that might be there.

She wondered what other creatures,
were lurking in the forest.
From the scariest and largest,
to the cutest and smallest.

The moon lit up the clear night sky,
casting shadows on the forest floor.
It hung suspended on nothing,
she'd never thought of that before.

Putting on her black woolen gloves,
Alexa looked for the branch of a tree.
To use as a kind of walking stick,
providing support for her journey.

She picked up her suitcase,
setting off again on her way.
One foot in front of the other,
through the snow and nature's decay.

Twigs and branches snapped beneath her,
with every step she'd take.
The cold December's icy chill,
caused her body to shiver and shake.

The tough terrain was hard going,
and seemed like it would never end.
Alexa felt desperately alone,
and wished she had a friend.

She began to recite her prayer,
but this time said it out loud.
Switching the case to her left hand,
wandering off, lonely as a cloud.

After a grueling two-hour trek,
Alexa needed to have a rest.
She was cold, tired, and hungry,
and definitely not at her best.

She found a thick fallen tree trunk,
where she was able to sit down.
Taking out the sandwiches she'd packed,
she placed them on the ground.

She hadn't brought anything to drink,
but wasn't overly worried.
She gathered up a handful of flakes,
fresh from recent snow flurries.

She placed them on her tongue,
letting it melt inside her mouth.
Not knowing where she was headed,
north, west, east, or south.

After she ate her sandwich,
and drank some water from the melted snow.
She noticed her feet needed attention,
before she could get back up and go.

She had some cuts on one of her legs,
and a hole in the sole of her shoe.
Without anything to repair the gash,
cold water kept seeping through.

She quickly rubbed her hands together,
trying to create some heat.
Then blew warm breath into her palms,
rubbing them against her feet.

After a short respite,
she continued on her way.
She was expected at the convent,
and didn't have time to delay.

She tried to remember the directions,
Herr Klauss had written in his note.
But as hard as she tried to remember,
she couldn't precisely recall what he'd wrote.

When she got to the end of the forest,
she crossed a field and a road nearby.
But couldn't remember which way to go,
as tears brimmed, ready to cry.

All of a sudden, from out of nowhere,
an old gentleman appeared through the frost.
"Good evening Frauline." He said to her,
"Can I help you, are you lost?"

Alexa was shocked by the man's appearance,
but was also relieved he was there.
He seemed like a sweet old grandfather,
with kind eyes and silvery white hair.

42

"Yes Sir, I'm lost,
and can't recall which way to go.
I've already walked for hours,
through the forest in the freezing snow."

The old man was empathetic,
and asked her desired destination.
When she told him the convent at Kreuzberg,
he said he'd guide her to its location.

The man suggested they stop for a rest,
on some logs by a frozen stream.
Alexa agreed it was a good idea,
sitting in the light of the moon's beam.

He opened up his bag,
and reached his hand down low.
He took out a bar of chocolate,
and snapped off the top row.

He then handed it to the stranger,
sitting by his side.
Alexa's face expressed emotions,
for once she didn't have to hide.

She placed the chocolate on her tongue,
and it slowly began to melt.
Releasing its flavors for her taste buds,
she'd forgotten how wonderful it felt.

The old man was delighted,
to see joy on the young girl's face.
He then handed her a bottle of milk,
and told her to have a taste.

"Thank you ever so much Sir,
you truly are so kind."
As she took a sip of the white liquid,
Bloomshen popped into her mind.

Alexa handed the man back his milk,
then put her arm around his shoulder.
"You are very welcome my dear.
I'm not usually much help, now I'm older."

"Well, this evening you've been my Angel,
my bright beacon in the dark of night.
If it wasn't for you guiding me,
I'd have taken the wrong road to the right."

"You've been the loveliest of company,
and I've enjoyed our interesting talk.
The milk and chocolate were delicious,
I feel all warmed up for the rest of our walk."

The old man was grateful,
for Alexa's true expressions of appreciation.
They were able to communicate freely,
without any age discrimination.

After they walked for a few more miles,
he said he'd be going in a different direction.
He began explaining which road she should take,
once Alexa reached the next intersection.

She thanked the old man, hugged him goodbye,
then he slowly turned and walked away.
Alexa was grateful for his offer of friendship,
and expressed it by beginning to pray.

It suddenly occurred to Alexa,
she'd forgotten to ask the man's name.
But he'd disappeared when she turned to ask,
and wondered if she'd gone insane.

He was there only a few seconds before,
and she knew he couldn't walk very fast.
She wondered if she'd perhaps imagined him,
but he wasn't around to ask.

She continued with her prayer of thanks,
directing it to God above.
"If he really was an Angel sent by you,
thank you for your perfect love."

~ 8 ~

ON A HOOK

The winter conditions worsened,
as a Baltic blizzard began to blow.
Alexa was tossed about in the wind,
and was soon knee-deep in snow.

She could hardly see in front of her,
reaching a small village on the way.
With almost total whiteout conditions,
Alexa searched for a place to stay.

She mustered up the courage,
and knocked on the first door she got to.
But it was dark and nobody answered,
or came to her rescue.

The third house which she tried,
had a light in the downstairs window.
She knocked on the black wooden door,
as the storm continued to blow.

A short German woman answered,
surprised to find Alexa there.
"What are you doing out here?" She asked,
pulling her in off the icy stair.

"I'm going to care for my aunt who's sick,
but the foul weather has slowed me down.
It's now too late to keep going,
I need a bed tonight in this town."

Suddenly, her curious husband appeared,
who was tall and rather fat.
As he slammed the outside door shut,
a hook revealed his German police hat.

"What is this all about?"
he insisted on being told.
"And why is this young woman,
standing here in my household?"

His wife said she was a good German girl,
on her way to see her sick aunt.
"But due to the bad weather and air strikes,
well, now, tonight, she can't."

"The war is the war," were his final few words,
then he disappeared to another room.
The woman apologized for her husband,
being the voice of doom and gloom.

Alexa couldn't believe she'd willingly,
walked to a German policeman's door.
His uniform displayed a swastika,
and she knew well what that stood for.

His wife invited her into the kitchen,
where she prepared Alexa a hot drink.
She was understandably apprehensive,
but was too frozen and exhausted to think.

After she warmed in front of the fire,
and got some heat back in her bones.
The woman showed her to a guest room,
where she'd spend the night in their home.

Alexa didn't now want to be there,
but it wasn't up for debate.
She lay on top of the bed,
knowing the hour was very late.

Alexa was overly anxious,
and couldn't find any peace.
She heard clatter from the kitchen,
making it impossible to sleep.

When Alexa went to investigate,
she overheard the woman cough.
She said she had to go be with her aunt,
and it was best she now headed off.

The woman made up a sandwich,
wrapped in paper with a slice of cake.
Alexa was in a rush to leave,
in case her husband might awake.

She made her way to the front door,
but still wasn't out of danger.
She was, however, grateful for,
the kindness of another stranger.

She put one foot in front of the other,
walking again on the snow-covered ground.
The dark country roads were deserted,
there wasn't a single soul around.

Finally, after a twenty-minute walk,
the convent came into her view.
She hoped for some more kindness,
from the nun whom Herr Klauss knew.

She walked up the long driveway,
and searched for a door to knock.
She knew it was now very late,
perhaps after one o'clock.

The chances of the nun being awake,
and waiting up were very slim.
But since Alexa had no other options,
she banged again on the knocker's rim.

Eventually the door was opened,
by a middle-aged nun dressed in black.
"Alexa? You're late you selfish girl."
"I'm terribly sorry," Alexa answered back.

She followed her into the building,
down a spiral staircase made of stone.
Along a dark hallway she was taken,
to an old dismal room on her own.

The nun had a candle in one hand,
and a large set of keys in the other.
She pointed to an old metal bed,
and ordered Alexa under the cover.

Alexa once again,
was shocked to her very core.
Then heard the distinctive noise,
of a key turning in the door.

"No, please don't lock me in!"
Alexa shouted through the door.
Which was a complete waste of time,
since the nun wasn't there anymore.

Resigned to the dire situation,
Alexa deeply felt defeat.
She curled up on top of the bed,
keeping her shoes on her frozen feet.

She reached her hand for her necklace,
which amazingly she'd managed to keep.
Then dozed off saying her prayer,
and finally fell asleep.

50

She woke early in the morning,
to the sound of keys turning in the lock.
There were no windows in the room,
resembling a cell from a prison block.

Two nuns stepped inside,
and told her it was time to start work.
Alexa was confused,
and interjected with a "But!"

"I'm only supposed to be here for one night,
then I'm finally going back home.
To be reunited with my mother and sister,
who was left in Poland alone."

The nuns laughed then threw down some clogs,
they showed absolutely no compassion.
"Hurry up and put them on,
haven't you heard? They're the latest fashion."

Alexa could tell their character,
was darker than their cloth.
She stood up from the old metal bed,
kicking her shoes defiantly off.

The moment was surreal,
pushing her feet in the oversized clogs.
Suddenly, in her memory,
she heard the bark of Herr Klauss's dogs.

She was taken to a large kitchen,
where nuns waited to be fed.
Then to a lonely table in the corner,
is where Alexa next was led.

She was given a bowl of porridge to eat,
and told to hurry up.
Then someone handed her lukewarm milk,
in an old, dented metal cup.

Two nuns marched Alexa,
to a cold room with a metal bath.
Deprived of any privacy,
she became the focus of their laugh.

They ordered her to strip naked,
and place her dirty clothes in a pile.
They seemed to take a sick pleasure,
as she shivered on the frozen tile.

At the same moment the nuns noticed,
the cross hanging from her neck.
Which had obviously been missed,
when the first nun forgot to check.

They told her to take it off,
or they'd remove it for her.
Alexa's heart sank to the floor,
her nightmare turned into horror.

Removing the necklace, she handed it over,
left with no other choice.
As she stepped into the bath of cold water,
a shriek escaped from her voice.

It was better to get the ordeal over with,
as fast as she possibly could.
She'd probably have to rely on them,
for her clothing, shelter, and food.

~ 9 ~

TWICE A SLAVE

Once dried and dressed in clean clothes,
Alexa was taken to the mother superior.
A mean-looking German woman,
who made others feel inferior.

She was then handed the necklace,
gifted to Alexa by her grandmother.
It was priceless and irreplaceable,
sentimentally there was no other.

She told Alexa if she did a good job,
she might get it back some day.
Then placed the chain around her own neck,
tucking the cross part away.

Alexa was determined,
to get her necklace back one day.
But she had to accept the fact,
for now that's where it would stay.

She was taken to her new place of work,
where she'd be washing piles of laundry.
And just like at the Klausses farmhouse,
she'd be forced to slave all day.

Finally, after dinner,
she was taken back to the cells.
But now there were some other girls,
imprisoned in the space as well.

Once the door was locked,
and the girls were together for the first time.
Alexa heard one of them say,
"You can sleep in that bed; this one's mine."

She politely said thank you,
and sat down on the vacant bed.
She kicked off her wooden clogs,
her feet were throbbing and red.

One of the girls began introducing them,
sharing their names, age, and nationality.
Alexa swapped her information,
realizing they all shared a commonality.

They were all blonde European girls,
who all had that Aryan look.
Each had been robbed of their families,
deprived of what Hitler's henchmen took.

Greta was Danish and the oldest,
at nineteen years of age.
Torn from her family at fourteen,
at night from the bed where she lay.

Marta was the youngest at seventeen,
and originally from Belgium.
Nazis barged in during family prayers,
killing her father and causing bedlam.

Henrietta, eighteen from Holland,
was also taken from her home.
But she chose not to share her story,
trying to handle her pain alone.

The girls finally got some sleep,
exhausted from their demanding chores.
They'd have to do it all again the next day,
when the key unlocked the door.

Early the next morning,
they woke to the sound of the door unlock.
The nuns arrived to collect them for work,
it was just approaching five o'clock.

After they'd finished eating breakfast,
the girls lingered on to overhear.
News reports on an old wireless radio,
saying "war's end was drawing near."

Masses of European and Jewish refugees,
were displaced across the country.
"Germans have a moral duty to help."
The reporter expressed rather bluntly.

The Mother Superior shouted out,
"That doesn't apply to you four."
Then two nuns escorted the girls,
and shuffled them out the door.

They were taken to the laundry room,
and immediately given their tasks.
She wondered if they'd to wash everything there,
but Alexa knew better than to ask.

Two of the girls were led away,
through an adjoining wooden door.
While Greta and Alexa began gathering,
piles of laundry off the floor.

Away in the far distance,
she heard an approaching plane.
Alexa remained vigilant,
while she tackled a stubborn stain.

Seconds later, an aircraft flew overhead,
and seemed to disappear.
But then the sound returned once more,
filling Alexa with dread and fear.

The whistling noise from a fast-falling bomb,
gave them little time to react.
Alexa dove under a large wooden table,
attempting to shelter from the impact.

The bomb hit its intended target,
destroying the convent's three buildings.
The damage was extensive,
as were the many killings.

A large stained-glass window shattered,
its shards flew around the space.
She buried herself in a pile of sheets,
which protected her body and face.

The table Alexa hid under,
snapped in half from the weight of debris.
She'd wisely crouched under its thick legs,
ensuring her relative safety.

The explosion was a violent one,
it produced a loud deafening sound.
Alexa was aware she couldn't hear,
as she stood up and spun around.

She scanned the immediate area,
and called out Greta's name.
But as Alexa listened for a reply,
nothing in return came.

Stepping over the strewn rubble,
she saw what she thought was a foot.
She could tell it wasn't Greta's,
by the fact it wore a black boot.

One of the nuns guarding her,
lay dead under a mound of stones.
The second one suffered the same fate,
there was no life left in her bones.

"Alexa, you're alive!" Greta shouted,
waiting for her friend to turn around.
But Alexa didn't respond,
due to the fact she had lost all sound.

Greta tapped her shoulder,
the girls embraced with a sigh of relief.
At the fact they had survived the bombing,
but had lost the clogs on their feet.

They immediately began searching,
but their friends were nowhere in sight.
Crawling through shattered broken walls,
they stepped out into the daylight.

The raw ruins of the convent,
lay bare on display.
The mangled bodies of deceased nuns,
lay rotting in decay.

Greta began to untie the lace,
on one of the dead nun's boots.
They would both now need a pair,
to make their escape on foot.

They heard a voice call from the rubble,
from someone who was buried alive.
Alexa struggled to reach her,
but unfortunately, the nun died.

As Alexa looked down and saw her face,
she discovered the woman's identity.
The mother superior who'd been so mean,
and first made them her enemy.

Alexa reached down to the woman's neck,
and began to undo the clasp.
"I did do a good job, now I'm taking this back!"
She'd recovered her necklace at last.

The familiar sound of a bomber's engine,
again began to fly near.
Greta pulled Alexa into some bushes,
realizing she still couldn't hear.

The airplane passed overhead,
without dropping another shell.
They wiped down their tattered clothes,
then Greta overheard someone yell.

"Well, aren't you two a sight for sore eyes?"
a female voice said in appreciation.
"Henrietta, thank God you're alive."
Greta replied in salutation.

A few seconds later behind Henrietta,
Marta appeared from the ruins.
She ran to join her three friends,
embraced in a joyful reunion.

Greta suggested they make their escape,
by taking two undamaged bikes.
They each wore a pair of dead nuns' boots,
heading off on their bicycle hike.

It was April 1945,
Alexa spent four months in that prison.
As the girls made their desperate escape,
freedom became their sole mission.

~ 10 ~

MAKING NEW DRESSES

Alexa never learned to ride a bike,
so Greta pedaled with her feet.
The other girls took turnabout,
sitting on the saddle's seat.

The road had an uneven surface,
making it hard for them to steer.
But as difficult as it was,
the girls all persevered.

They stopped along the roadway,
across from a bombed-out house.
They searched inside for crumbs of food,
left behind by a hasty mouse.

Marta and Henrietta went to explore,
the garden at the rear.
Alexa and Greta entered the house,
as an army truck drove near.

They were ordered out with their hands up,
while soldiers aimed their weapons.
Alexa's face displayed fear,
not hiding her expressions.

They were both loaded into the truck,
and speedily driven away.
They didn't ask about anyone else,
and neither girl chose to say.

The truck with captured locals inside,
drove to an abandoned German school.
Locked up with a few hundred prisoners,
Alexa wondered why life was so cruel.

They were forced to sit on the floor of the gym,
all just a few feet apart.
And every few hours ten women were chosen,
by soldiers to depart.

There was nothing to eat or drink,
all they could do was sit and stare.
Alexa felt her blood boil inside,
then announced she shouldn't be there.

"I'm not a German, there's been a mistake,
I was taken from Poland as a slave."
An Allied soldier removed her from the gym,
and said, "Smart move, that was brave."

She met with the US Commander,
in charge of the Allied operation.
She began telling her story,
from capture through liberation.

The Commander was empathetic,
and had food brought for her to digest.
He moved her to a smaller room,
where she'd get a more comfortable rest.

Alexa took a bar of the chocolate,
asking it be given to her Belgian friend.
Marta was soon freed to join her,
on Alexa's loyalty, she could depend.

There were other freed European women,
sitting in the room where they were.
It was clear they too had suffered hardships,
misery, loss, and despair.

The next day a soldier took Alexa back,
to the gym full of German prisoners.
He told her to randomly select ten women,
from the group of Nazi conspirators.

Alexa was reluctant at first,
but eventually selected them all.
Soldiers marched them out of the gym,
across the road towards the schoolhouse wall.

Alexa had to supervise their work,
like a boss giving them strict orders.
Now on manual labor clean-up duty,
she made sure they didn't cut corners.

Two soldiers again took Alexa away,
this time to a nearby church.
She began to ask what was happening,
but the soldiers wouldn't say very much.

They led her to the altar,
and the vestibule just behind.
As she entered the small room,
the view that unfolded blew her mind.

There were many priceless treasures gathered,
and a large collection of valuables stored.
Alexa was told to choose anything she wished,
from the confiscated Nazi-stolen hoard.

"No, I can't," she said,
"because it isn't mine to take."
The soldiers began to laugh,
but Alexa wasn't being fake.

She was honest, with integrity,
which she was unwilling to betray.
She knew it'd been stolen from people like her,
when they were forcefully taken away.

The soldiers said it was their Commander,
who'd insisted she pick something for herself.
Looking again, she spied a roll of material,
resting against an ornate shelf.

"How about some of this?
I'd like to make a new dress.
My own clothes are tattered and torn,
I'm sure I must look a mess."

"I only need about twenty yards,
can you please cut the length for me?"
One of the soldiers took out his knife,
and said, "Sure, that'll be easy."

They returned Alexa to the school room,
with the rolled-up section of material.
"Look girls, we can sew ourselves a new dress,
there's enough to make one for us all."

The women were delighted,
that's how they spent their next few days.
Folding, cutting, and sewing together,
bonding in therapeutic ways.

It was announced they'd finally be leaving,
to a camp for people who were displaced.
A truck would depart for France,
leaving Germany in haste.

There was one last act of kindness,
the commander wanted to do.
The soldier he sent to the school gym,
returned with two pairs of women's shoes.

Alexa was surprised by the kindness,
of the Commander's thoughtful gesture.
Both girls kicked off the old boots,
slipping their new shoes on with pleasure.

Thanking the stranger for his kindness,
she hadn't known three days before.
Alexa was convinced she'd remember him,
in her mind forever more.

The truck exited the school gates,
with the women loaded in the rear.
Alexa waved goodbye to the commander,
but she didn't shed a tear.

The road ahead was fraught with danger,
they risked being discovered on route.
Two soldiers with rifles travelled with them,
locked and loaded, and ready to shoot.

The truck needed to refuel,
after hours of driving on the road.
It stopped at an army fill-up point,
where the women began to unload.

Their presence and prettiness was noticed,
by the Allied troops when they arrived.
They hovered around them like vultures,
eyeing up who was still alive.

One Italian soldier in particular,
tried to win Alexa's favor.
He started to play his guitar,
and romantically serenade her.

Alexa blushed in embarrassment,
at being the recipient of his song.
When he got to the familiar chorus,
some of the others sang along.

He seemed totally smitten by Alexa,
staring into her eyes of deep blue.
He then handed her his guitar,
and said, "Amore' this is for you."

Alexa was taken by surprise,
she didn't quite know what to say.
Then she innocently blurted out,
"But I don't know how to play."

"Never mind, you can trade it in France,"
said a woman standing close by.
And as the truck slowly began to drive off,
the Italian soldier blew a kiss goodbye.

~ 11 ~

NEW ADMIRERS

The truck finally arrived in Mourmelon,
at a displacement camp run by the Red Cross.
Freed prisoners trying to get back home,
carried deep scars of pain and loss.

Marta and Alexa registered their details,
and were given something to eat and drink.
When suddenly in the canteen, Marta said,
"Is that actually who I think?"

Alexa turned around,
and there stood Henrietta.
Marta was standing next to her,
which made everything so much better.

They were allocated bunks together,
inside of a woman's dorm.
At least by being all together,
there'd be less chance of any harm.

A female officer arranged for Alexa,
to sell her guitar to a soldier she knew.
Reasoning, that in the dorm it'd be stolen,
better to get a dollar or two.

They didn't have many possessions,
only some ragged and old worn clothes.
Except for Marta and Alexa,
who wore the new dresses they'd sewed.

Given American Red Cross uniforms,
to wear at work each day.
Their jobs would be in the laundry house,
that's how they'd pay their way.

Camp life was a group effort,
everyone was given a job to complete.
Hygiene was essential,
supplying clean clothes, towels, and sheets.

The women washed, soaked, and scrubbed,
cleaning piles of never-ending laundry.
But this time they weren't forced slaves,
this time their hard work was voluntary.

Three of the women borrowed bicycles,
on a scorching French July day.
It was time Alexa learned to ride a bike,
and when she got her first taste of hay.

They cycled to a country field,
and lay in the long, tall grass.
Promising they'd be friends forever,
or as long as their lives would last.

70

They steered downhill towards a village,
once back on the roadway.
But Alexa hadn't learned to use the brakes,
and a large obstacle stood in her way.

Unable to slow down her bike,
or bring it to a stop safely.
She flew headfirst over the handlebars,
into a huge stack of fresh hay.

Her friends were laughing hysterically,
at the scene they had just witnessed.
When an American soldier came to her aid,
retrieving her bike, now slightly twisted.

He checked that Alexa was okay,
and seemed relieved she wasn't hurt.
She tried to act like nothing happened,
straightening up, wiping off the dirt.

Her two girlfriends parked their bikes,
against the wall of a local café.
They sat down at an outdoor table,
soaking up the sun's warm rays.

"I'm Mark, a soldier from Brooklyn.
What's your name, Mademoiselle?"
Alexa answered his questions,
giving her pertinent intel.

71

"Would you like to join me for a drink?
I'd like to talk with you some more.
I've noticed you back at the camp,
but we've never spoken before."

Alexa was flattered by his interest,
but was slightly embarrassed too.
As she politely accepted his invitation,
he wheeled her bike to join the other two.

The waitress served two cokes,
while they sat in conversation.
Mark asked if she'd like to go on a date,
and worked on his powers of persuasion.

Alexa had never been on a date,
nor had a real romantic interest before.
There were many things she'd never experienced,
but didn't want a life like that anymore.

Not wanting to appear overly eager,
she resisted agreeing to the date.
Alexa said she would think about it,
and Mark said he would wait.

The girls said goodbye and cycled back,
as the sun was beginning to set.
Greta asked if she'd be dating Mark,
but Alexa hadn't decided yet.

Once they arrived back at the camp,
they told Marta about their fun day.
Of the rescue by an American,
after crashing into a stack of hay.

The women were in fits of laughter,
at the retelling of their friend's mishap.
And about her new romantic admirer,
wearing an American Army cap.

After sunrise and breakfast,
the women headed off to work.
Mountains of laundry awaited,
for the women to remove the dirt.

Unusually, a selection was made,
two women were moved to new positions.
They were taken to the storehouse,
a job with much easier conditions.

"I hope you can both count and write."
Said the officer with a questioning look.
Their new job was to count boxes of soap,
and write numbers in a large book.

It certainly wasn't stressful,
and the soaps had a pleasant smell.
The girls were rather pleased,
things had worked out for them so well.

Two male electricians arrived,
to repair a broken light.
The blond one climbed up a ladder,
keeping the women in his sight.

Every now and then,
Alexa caught his eye in a glance.
And for the very first time felt as though,
she was actually in a trance.

She tried to not keep looking,
or be caught by his handsome stare.
But the very next thing she knew,
he was standing right there.

"Bonjour Mademoiselle, my name's Antoni,
may I ask please, what is yours?"
Alexa tried to find the mask,
to come across all calm and mature.

She said her name was Alexa,
and blushed all the while as she did.
She was now a vibrant young woman,
but felt more like an awkward kid.

"I'd remember if I'd seen you before,"
he said with a flirtatious smile.
When did you start working here,
have you been here for a while?"

Alexa shook her head 'no',
that it was actually her first shift.
Antoni smiled his blue eyes and said,
"Then you are my lucky gift."

"You're a very beautiful woman,
and you smell like fine perfume.
"Don't be silly," Alexa said,
"it's just the odor of soap in this room."

"Will you meet me after work Alexa,
so we can get to know each other better?"
Antoni wasn't shy in coming forward,
he was quite the go-getter.

Alexa wouldn't be pressured,
and said she had to meet her two friends.
Antoni wouldn't take no for an answer,
so she agreed to the next day in the end.

Antoni returned to his repair,
climbing back up the ladder nearby.
He'd managed to take her breath away,
and she now felt her first butterfly.

The afternoon passed by quickly,
as the girls packed soaps away.
"Hello pretty lady, do you like your new job?"
Alexa heard a familiar voice say.

"Hello Mark, what are you doing here?"
she said to the soldier from the day before.
Just then, Antoni dropped a tool from his hand,
making a loud crash as it hit the floor.

It was probably done on purpose,
to disrupt their conversation.
But it didn't seem to work,
and Mark continued his declaration.

"This is a coincidence," Alexa said,
"I've now seen you twice in two days."
"I just stopped by to see if the jobs I arranged,
had worked out for you okay."

"Thank you very much Mark,
what a thoughtful thing to do."
"Well, I figured it'd be easier work,
and that you'd both be good at it too."

He asked if she'd decided on their date,
but she now had a new romantic interest.
Alexa couldn't mask her true feelings,
nor decide what to do for the best.

Her friend Henrietta bailed her out,
inventing an excuse to call her away.
Mark was also persistent,
and said he'd ask her again the next day.

76

Not used to having so much attention,
thrown in her direction.
Alexa became confused,
finding it hard to make her selection.

As the work shift neared its end,
Antoni packed away their things.
Walking over to Alexa, he begged,
"Meet me tomorrow, let's see what life brings."

They met up with Marta and Greta,
at the end of their long workday.
Henrietta told of Alexa's new admirer,
now there were two of them in play.

The girls joked and giggled,
cracking a few teasing friendly jokes.
"Did you get butterflies in your belly,
and did your heart skip a beat when he spoke?"

"I think I did," she said,
"but I didn't know what they were at the time."
They laughed like giddy schoolgirls,
while Henrietta did a butterfly mime.

They walked back to their dorm room,
and climbed into their bunks.
Where they continued to question Alexa,
about her two tall, handsome hunks.

Alexa answered their questions,
then she lay down and said her prayer.
Hoping that her mother and sister,
were doing the same thing, somewhere.

~ 12 ~

KALEIDOSCOPE OF BUTTERFLIES

The next day after work ended,
Alexa let down her hair for a change.
She tried to look her very best,
for meeting Antoni as arranged.

He was waiting outside patiently,
exactly on the hour.
Then pulled out from behind his back,
a yellow rose in a bunch of wildflowers.

He presented them to Alexa,
briefly touching her soft hand.
A kaleidoscope of butterflies fluttered inside,
way too excited to land.

He took her for a long walk,
through the surrounding countryside.
Then he chose an old oak tree,
for them to sit down beside.

He lay his jacket on the grass,
so Alexa could sit down.
Then took out a bar of chocolate,
placing the wrapper on the ground.

He broke off some pieces,
and told her to take a bite.
Her memory drifted back,
to the old man, on that winter's night.

Antoni was curious,
as to what she was thinking about.
And that's when she began telling him,
how her war years had turned out.

"That's quite a harrowing story,
you've really been through a lot."
"Yes, but I've been more fortunate than others,
who were beaten, tortured, and shot."

Antoni seemed uncomfortable,
and lit up another cigarette.
Almost, as if there was something,
he was trying hard to forget.

"I believe God was my protector,
it was Him who kept me safe.
And for that I thank my Babcia and mother,
for planting the seeds of my faith."

"Your way works for you Alexa,
and I wish I had such a faith."
But to be really honest with you,
I don't like religion's taste."

"It's true, religion causes many problems,
and makes hypocrites out of men.
But remember God Almighty created us,
and will repay our loyalty, in the end."

Alexa reached for more chocolate,
Antoni was unconvinced by her sermon.
She asked him to tell his story,
of how he was captured by the Germans.

He said he was born in Gryfów Śląski,
when it was taken as German land.
"My family moved to the city of Łódź,
where my grandfather's empire was planned."

His family owned five factories,
until the restrictions of the Nazi's evil laws.
When they confiscated Polish businesses,
without giving legitimate cause.

"They took over our five factories,
using them for their war machine needs.
We were stripped of our valuable possessions,
our assets used for wicked deeds."

"My father was forced to work in the ghetto,
handing out ration cards to Polish Jews.
He gave extra cards to families with small children.
and for his kindness, his freedom he'd lose."

"That was the last time I saw him,
the day he was arrested at work.
My mother was told by a neighbor,
the Gestapo loaded him onto a truck."

Alexa was visibly saddened,
hearing Antoni's emotional outpour.
He sat next to her on the grass,
and continued talking some more.

Alexa reached for his forearm,
but Antoni abruptly pulled it away.
Which took her completely by surprise,
not knowing what for the best she should say.

Antoni pulled up his shirt sleeve,
revealing scars on his upper arm.
"Oh, I'm so sorry, what happened to you?
How did you come to such harm?"

"I did it!" He said, to Alexa's amazement,
"the best thing I could think of at the time.
I created myself a good excuse,
so I wouldn't have to kill on the frontline."

"I was forced to join the German army,
and in that I had no say.
I had to follow the orders,
the Nazis made us obey."

82

"I made the decision to cut my own arm,
so I'd be registered as unfit for combat.
I was listed as seriously wounded,
and instead given an electrician's hat."

"So you see, it worked out very nicely,
doing things my way.
Because it was that electricity,
which brought us together yesterday."

The butterflies fluttered in Alexa's heart,
as his words lingered and stuck.
That was the very moment,
she knew Cupid's arrow had struck.

Antoni leaned forward,
and delivered Alexa's first kiss.
She felt the electricity spark,
as her soft young lips touched his.

It lasted a few short seconds,
then Antoni pulled back, letting go.
"Promise me you'll keep my secret,
we can't let anyone else know."

"No one can know I'm geographically German,
they wouldn't understand.
I'm as good as any other Polish man,
Poland is my true homeland."

"Yes, I'll keep your secret."
then he leaned in for another kiss.
Alexa felt deliriously happy,
'This must be love, I've never felt like this.'

"Will you be my girl, Alexa?
Please say that you'll be mine."
"Yes, I'll be your girlfriend Antoni,
no need to ask a second time."

He held her in his tight embrace,
as the sun set in the crimson sky.
Stroking her long blonde hair,
as a flock of geese overhead flew by.

He suggested they head back to the camp,
it was already way past dinner time.
But neither of them felt hungry,
due to love's distraction in their minds.

They walked back together hand in hand,
arranging to meet again the next day.
He gave her a kiss good night,
then watched his new girlfriend walk away.

Her three friends waited in their bunks,
for Alexa to return from her date.
They were anxious to hear of her new romance,
and could no longer patiently wait.

"Alexa's in love…" Marta sang,
noticing her radiant glow.
"So what if I am?" She said,
happy to let them all know.

"You better tell poor Mark," Said Greta,
"he came by earlier asking where you were.
When I told him you were out with Antoni,
I think I heard his heart tear."

"Oh, please don't say he's miserable,
I couldn't bear that.
But it's not like we were dating,
I'm not some two-timing rat."

They asked a lot of questions,
and she did her honest best to reply.
She remembered to keep Antoni's promise,
but to her friends she wouldn't lie.

After a while lying in her bunk,
she realized she'd left her flowers behind.
She began retracing her steps,
through the footprints of her mind.

~ 13 ~

GOING HOME, ALONE

Another workday dawned in the camp,
just like they had for five months prior.
They longed to return home to their families,
but the post-war situation remained dire.

A soldier came looking for Henrietta,
with news of a Dutch transportation truck.
Some refugees were leaving in the morning,
and from the list, he said she was in luck.

She returned to her workstation,
and told Alexa the good news.
But instead of elation and excitement,
they both had the blues.

"I'm going to miss you more than you know,"
tears brimmed in Alexa's eyes.
"Life won't be the same without you my friend,"
tears trickled, and Henrietta cried.

"We better go find Marta and Greta,
I wonder if they are leaving too?"
They went to search for their friends,
and information from someone who knew.

When they finally found one another,
no one else had been notified to leave.
They skipped work to spend time with Henrietta,
but her leaving filled them with grief.

They headed towards the French countryside,
to an open field full of flowers.
Reminiscing on their time spent together,
the four friends chatted for hours.

They vowed that no matter what,
in contact they'd always stay.
They would remain best friends forever,
until they were old and gray.

When they returned to the dorm,
there was a note on Greta's bed.
She was to report to the main office,
but that was all that it said.

They looked at each other in silence,
already guessing what it meant.
Thankfully they'd stolen their last day,
which had not been misspent.

They made their way to the canteen,
it would be their last meal together.
Antoni arrived looking for his girl,
and Alexa introduced him to the others.

"Why did you stand me up Alexa,
and not meet me as we planned?"
She explained her best friends were leaving,
to return to their homeland.

He said he understood,
but asked if they could meet up later that night.
Alexa politely declined and said,
"I need to be with my friends tonight."

Antoni wasn't happy,
but there was nothing he could do.
He didn't like not getting his own way,
or being sent to the back of the queue.

The four friends made their way to the dorm,
for their final night sleeping there.
Alexa had them kneel beside her,
and began to recite her prayer.

Early the next morning,
the sun was beginning to rise.
Which wasn't clearly visible,
due to thick clouds and dark gray skies.

Henrietta and Greta gathered their things,
for the long-distance journey ahead.
"Is anyone else going to Belgium?"
The French soldier who was driving said.

Marta answered she was Belgian,
but no one had informed her to leave.
The soldier confirmed she was on his list.
"I don't have my things, can you wait, please?

He said he'd give her ten minutes,
to run and fetch her belongings.
Alexa ran back with Marta,
as her new reality was dawning.

Her three friends were leaving,
they were finally all going home.
But sadly, Alexa wasn't,
she'd have to stay in the camp alone.

The truck's engine revved in the rain,
as they shared their final parting embrace.
They waved to Alexa, blowing kisses in the wind,
as tears rolled down her face.

Her friends were gone in an instant,
once again she was all alone.
As she walked to the storehouse she thought,
'I've got through worse days than this on my own.'

After her shift was over,
she met Antoni as planned.
Alexa broke down in tears,
and fell into his comforting arms.

Antoni was supportive,
and held her trembling body tight.
"Don't worry, you've got me darling,
I'll make sure that you're all right."

Consumed by her sadness,
but strengthened by Antoni's support.
The two became inseparable,
with him her new beacon of hope.

Before the official end of the war,
some released prisoners tried to return.
To the lives which were wrenched from them,
and their need to create a new one.

To find what was lost or stolen,
to recover what was left behind.
To reunite with friends and relatives,
whose memory burned bright in their minds.

They shared many conversations,
planning their journey back to Poland.
It wasn't quite so daunting,
now she had Antoni holding her hand.

On the last Friday in September,
he suggested they watch the setting sun.
He took her back to the old oak tree,
where their romance had first begun.

It was only two months earlier,
when they'd had their first date.
Their relationship flourished fast,
but he no longer wanted to wait.

Remembering the flowers she'd left behind,
she began looking all around.
She found some withered remnants,
lying strewn on the sun-scorched ground.

Antoni politely excused himself,
saying he'd be right back.
Then disappeared behind the oak tree,
and off the beaten track.

When he returned, he had fresh flowers,
this time a red rose in the center of the bouquet.
He presented them to his girlfriend,
then taking her hand he proceeded to say.

"Alexa, will you marry me?
I want you to be my wife."
He reached into his pocket,
retrieving his temporary token of life.

He handed her a rounded piece of wire,
with a red and clear bead threaded through.
I'm sorry this ring is only handmade,
but it's the best that I could do."

"Yes Antoni, I'll marry you."
Alexa didn't need time to consider.
Neither for that matter did Antoni,
as he leaned in and kissed her.

Against the background of a crimson sky,
a flock of geese flew above.
Alexa's heart helplessly became,
engulfed in the flames of love.

They could now make real plans,
and focus on their future.
Antoni said he'd take care of everything,
of that she could be sure.

They walked back to the camp,
after the sun had faded from sight.
Stars sparkled like perfect diamonds,
against the blanket of dark velvet night.

He told her he'd saved some money,
from all his poker game winnings.
Which would at least give them a small start,
financing their marital beginnings.

"We're getting married and finally going home."
Her excitement beamed ecstatically.
"Yes beautiful, we are." He confirmed,
then they kissed goodnight automatically.

The next morning, he visited the camp's priest,
who agreed to officiate on the day.
At the station he enquired about train tickets,
to Paris and Berlin, but only one way.

Antoni knew a French jeweler in town,
who gave him a deal on two wedding rings.
He said his wife could style Alexa's hair,
as she was a hairdresser, amongst other things.

Antoni proudly reported back to Alexa,
on the results of his productive day.
The plans were set in motion,
they'd be married the following Saturday.

She returned to her empty bunk,
wishing her friends were there to share.
But her three best friends were gone,
alone again she said her prayer.

~ 14 ~

PARIS HONEYMOON

The week flew by very quickly,
the following day they'd be wed.
She agreed to the kindness of the stranger,
who offered a free hairstyle for her head.

They walked together to the jeweler's shop,
where the two women were introduced.
The men politely excused themselves,
while Sonia explained the styles she produced.

She showed her some temporary hair dyes,
the latest thing on Paris's fashion scene.
Alexa liked the idea of a new look,
and from the colors, chose bottle B-13.

A couple of hours later,
the men returned to the shop.
But when Antoni saw Alexa,
his face displayed shock.

"Wow, what have you done,
and where is my pretty blonde?"
Alexa's happy smile dropped,
before she could even respond.

"It's the latest style in Paris,
and I felt like I needed a change.
So I selected dark brown,
from the brand new color range."

"Don't worry said Sonia,
it'll soon wash out and be gone."
"Good!" Said Antoni,
"because I only love blondes."

Later she told him she loved him,
and asked if he loved her too.
To which he sarcastically answered,
"Sure, I love both of you."

He laughed out loud as he said it,
but Alexa didn't find the fun.
"What more could a man ask for?
Getting two wives for the price of one."

"You better behave yourself Antoni,
or you'll end up with none."
"You're more than enough for me Alexa,
our journey has just begun."

She chose not to wear the old wedding dress,
which the Red Cross loaned to new brides.
Instead, she wore her smart uniform,
to match Antoni's, standing by her side.

He promised they'd have a proper wedding,
   when they finally got back home.
With friends, family, decorations,
   and a new wedding dress of her own.

The hour arrived to say their vows,
   exchange rings and say, "I do."
They promised to love one another,
   in a bond and union between only two.

They sealed the proceedings with a kiss,
   and signed their marriage paper.
An Allied soldier with an old camera,
   took their photo as a special favor.

The formalities were over quickly,
   and the newlyweds began their new life.
They were congratulated around the camp,
   as the handsome husband and beautiful wife.

Later in the canteen,
   an impromptu party began.
The US soldier who'd bought her guitar,
   played music and also sang.

One soldier brought a bottle of vodka,
   another brought a bottle of wine.
A small cake was made by the cook,
   and everyone had a good time.

It helped make their wedding more special,
receiving such kindness from strangers.
Especially under such turbulent times,
still at high risk from post-war dangers.

They left the party at 9 o'clock,
due to an early departure in the morning.
They could hitch a ride to Paris by truck,
a soldier had just informed them.

They spent their first night together,
sleeping in each other's arms.
For the first time she felt truly safe,
like she'd never come to more harm.

The drive to the Capital was a peaceful one,
they sat up front for the first time.
The driver said he'd have them in Paris,
arriving just before nine.

He took them on the scenic route,
with Paris's architectural beauty on display.
Driving around the Arc De Triomphe
and down the Champs Élysées.

He slowly drove them along,
the banks of the river Seine.
Past the Louvre Museum,
and Cathedral of Norte Dame.

They continued traveling southwards,
towards the Eiffel Tower.
Then on to the Gare Du Nord Station,
exactly ten minutes, before the ninth hour.

They thanked the driver, who said 'Bon Voyage',
Antoni carried their duffle bag.
The train to Berlin wasn't till one o'clock,
which was the only little snag.

As they walked through the railway station,
a real tapestry of humanity was on display.
A mix of soldiers and civilians,
young and old, blonde, and gray.

She saw the rich and the poor,
the injured and the maimed.
Alexa thought about how God,
had created them all the same.

Each of them had different stories,
etched upon their face.
Some with pain and scars,
some with elegance and grace.

Parisians in matching French fashions,
handbags, hats, and high heels.
Smart Businessmen in tailored suits,
traveling to seal their next deal.

Rough-looking men in ragged clothing,
mere mortals in gaunt-looking shells.
Their hollow faces and sunken eyes,
betrayed their unspoken hells.

Antoni next suggested,
they find a Parisian café.
They walked together hand in hand,
enjoying the sights along the way.

'We're technically on our honeymoon,'
Alexa glanced down at her wedding ring.
'And we are actually here in the city of love,
which in itself, is an amazing thing.'

The streets of Paris were beautiful,
the ornate buildings set the scene.
Painted wooden window shutters,
with flower boxes in between.

Tables and chairs sat outside street cafés,
where neighbors and friends gathered to mix.
Or read the latest newspaper story,
while getting their black caffeine fix.

Antoni selected a small café,
and said he had enough francs.
For a hot drink and fresh pastry each,
and it wouldn't break the bank.

For the first time in her adult life,
she truly felt happy and free.
And was finally with someone,
whom she actually wanted to be.

This was a fresh new chapter,
in her no longer lonely life.
Alexa was the leading lady,
she was Antoni's new wife.

They stopped at the butchers' and bakers',
to buy some food supplies for the train.
Antoni carried the packages,
walking back to the station again.

Alexa was distracted by the contents,
in the window of an old bookshop.
By the same Polish Bible she'd read as a child,
so she asked Antoni if they could stop.

Inside was an old French gentleman,
in the Bible she turned to Psalm 91.
She began to read the words in Polish,
which ran straight off her tongue.

The old man's eyes lit up,
he asked her to read it louder.
She spoke the familiar words clearer,
and not once did she flounder.

"How much for the old Bible Monsieur?
I'd like to buy it for my wife."
"Well since she reads it so beautifully,
it's my gift, as a guide for her life."

He said his own grandmother was Polish,
and had once owned the same Bible too.
He told her to take it back to Poland,
"Read it often, let its words walk with you."

Alexa was overcome with emotions,
"Thank you Sir, this means more than you know."
She leaned over kissing his round, rosy cheeks,
and then they said cheerio.

Alexa was delighted,
by the kindness of yet another stranger.
She always believed in good,
and wouldn't let people's hate, change her.

~ 15 ~

TRAIN TO BERLIN

They arrived back at the station,
and headed for platform five.
Steam billowed from the engine,
as the Berlin train arrived.

Its brakes screeched loudly piercing the air,
its speed reduced, then completely stopped.
Down the arriving passengers jumped,
up to the train, new passengers hopped.

Antoni found an empty compartment,
which had no one sitting inside.
He loaded their things up onto a shelf,
preparing for their long train ride.

The station master blew his whistle,
and the train began to increase speed.
"We are finally going home my darling."
"At last," sighed Alexa in relief.

Soon after their departure,
a train conductor asked to see their tickets.
Alexa's memories wandered back,
while Antoni searched his pockets.

"You look very serious, Alexa,
what are you thinking about?"
"My last train ride to Berlin,
and how different it could have all turned out."

She told him about the first-class ticket,
Herr Klauss gave to make her getaway.
"In a carriage full of Nazi soldiers,
I fooled them all, let's just say."

Antoni was impressed,
as his wife told her riveting story.
Then she gave all thanks for her escape,
to her Bible and God's glory.

Antoni had no faith in God,
but he respected Alexa's belief.
She cuddled in close to his chest,
and they both drifted off to sleep.

Alexa woke a few hours later,
and began preparing some food.
Baguettes, cheese, sausage, and some milk,
filled their stomachs and tasted good.

About an hour or so later,
they arrived at Frankfurt's main station.
Antoni jumped outside for a smoke,
while they finished their conversation.

The station master blew his whistle,
Antoni stepped back onto the train.
He slid the compartment door open,
to find a woman sat across from them.

She stared out of the window,
as the train went speeding by.
Reluctant to connect or speak,
not looking them in the eye.

She sat as if in a trance,
clutching a brown paper bag on her knee.
Alexa took out her Bible,
deciding to pass the time, she'd read.

Antoni went to the restaurant car,
saying he'd be back in a little while.
He kissed his wife on her cheek,
which filled her face with a smile.

He walked through the train's carriages,
towards the restaurant car.
Scanning the scene around him,
he ordered a beer from the bar.

He spotted some Allied soldiers,
at a nearby table playing cards.
Then moved to a seat near them,
overhearing, from just a few yards.

Antoni wasn't shy in coming forward,
and was invited to join their poker game.
He made out he was a beginner,
when he introduced himself and his name.

He said he had some francs remaining,
and fancied seeing how his luck would ride.
He told them he had just gotten married,
to his beautiful blonde Polish bride.

He threw his money into the pot,
and was dealt a hand of cards.
He made some subtle, deliberate moves,
choosing winning cards to discard.

Antoni lost the first hand,
which the soldiers were happy to win.
He also lost the next two,
before he started reeling them in.

Putting on his poker face,
the following game was his first win.
He placed his winnings on the next hand,
then said, he was all in.

His plan worked, winning the soldier's money,
then he announced that he was done.
But the soldiers wanted a chance to win back,
their cash which he'd just won.

He told them he'd go check on his wife,
just to keep her sweet.
Then he'd return to play some more cards,
but little did they know, he'd cheat.

When he returned to the compartment,
the scene hadn't really changed.
Alexa was still reading her Bible,
the other woman still acted strange.

He told Alexa he'd been playing cards,
winning money from a few good hands.
He asked if he could return to play,
telling her he had some big plans.

"Why not keep the money we have,
rather than risk losing it on a dumb bet?"
He knew she had a very valid point.
"Yes, sometimes Alexa, but not yet."

"I cast out my net and they took the bait,
that's when they thought I couldn't play.
But they bit, and now I have them hooked,
trust me, we'll be the big winners today."

Alexa returned to reading her Bible,
while Antoni went back to the card game.
The strange woman continued staring blankly,
out the window of the moving train.

Alexa reached for her bag,
taking out chocolate and the milk.
She longed for the taste in her mouth,
of that smooth melting texture like silk.

She asked the woman if she'd like some,
but oddly, she didn't reply.
Alexa asked in Polish a second time,
that's when the woman began to cry.

Alexa moved over beside her,
putting her arm on the woman's shoulder.
Tenderly being compassionate,
like a loving aunt, who was older.

"I didn't mean to make you cry,
I was only trying to be kind.
Sadly, you look like a poor soul,
with too much pain in her mind."

"I just thought you might like some chocolate,
it always helps to cheer up my mind."
The woman cried some more, then said,
"It's been so long since anyone's been this kind."

Alexa offered the woman some milk,
who reached into the bag she'd been holding.
She pulled out an old, dented metal cup,
which had lost most of its enamel coating.

"Look, I have my own cup,
I always have it ready."
Alexa filled it halfway up,
trying to keep her hand steady.

After drinking the milk,
she wiped the cup dry on her sleeve.
As she went to put it away,
Alexa said, "Have some more, please."

After some milk and chocolate,
Alexa asked the woman her name.
"I used to be called Teressa,
before replaced with a number of shame."

Next, Teressa began to tell,
of the nightmare she'd gone through.
And how inhumanely she'd been treated,
simply for being a Jew.

"I was rounded up in Kraków at gunpoint,
with my family in the street.
Then crammed into filthy boxcars like animals,
forced to stand the whole way on our feet."

"We were transported to hell on earth,
and separated that very day.
I've never before told anyone,
these things I'm about to say."

"They took my belongings, they took my clothes,
they even took my shoes.
Everything that was precious and dear to me,
they made sure I would lose."

"They took my wedding ring, they took my hair,
by shaving it off my head.
They took my husband, parents and two children,
whom I now believe to be dead."

She lifted up her left sleeve,
revealing a tattoo etched in her skin.
"They took my name and my identity,
and instead, carved this number in."

"It was desperate and demoralizing,
every second of every day.
I became convinced there was no God,
and refused anymore to pray."

"Crammed into disgusting barracks,
with hundreds of wretched strangers.
We were constantly under threat,
never free from the camp's dangers."

"The bunks were filled beyond capacity,
with six or eight women in each bed.
There were no blankets or mattresses,
and no pillows for our heads."

"We were beaten and starved,
and treated worse than dogs.
Forced to work hard labor,
in old, oversized, wooden clogs."

"A constant target for random bullets,
from any soldier's gun.
In a split second, for no reason at all,
they'd shoot just about anyone."

Alexa was moved by Teressa's account,
tears trickled from her eyes.
She now understood the woman's behavior,
which no longer wore a disguise.

Alexa gave a brief synopsis.
of what she'd suffered during the war.
She told it like a newspaper report,
more factual than emotionally raw.

"I hope you find your mother and sister,
and that they're both still alive."
She'd never accepted the possibility,
that they hadn't actually survived.

After their floods of emotions released,
they returned back to silence once more.
The woman stared out the window again,
and Alexa read her Bible as before.

Teressa stood up suddenly,
and said she had to go.
Alexa assumed she went to the toilet,
but she never returned to the window.

Antoni returned to the compartment,
to tell Alexa of his big win.
He wrapped his arm around her shoulder,
and his wife tightly cuddled in.

~ 16 ~

TRAIN TO WARSAW

They arrived in Berlin late evening,
the Warsaw train was due at midnight.
A guard said it wouldn't go the whole way,
due to Warsaw's becoming a bomb site.

They found an empty compartment,
once they boarded the Warsaw train.
For two long day's journey,
it would be their new domain.

Antoni had promised his wife,
they'd get a drink in the restaurant car.
Alexa ordered a black coffee,
while he opted for a beer from the bar.

The newlyweds discussed their future,
and their excitement of returning home.
They also agreed it was far better,
they were not going back alone.

The sun began to rise over Warsaw,
as the train drew closer to the city.
But the images that came into view,
were far from looking pretty.

Destruction filled the landscape,
as far as their eyes could see.
Row after row of burnt-out ruins,
resembling an apocalyptic catastrophe.

Half-standing bomb-blasted buildings,
with walls and roofs blown out.
Mangled metal, mounds of bricks,
and splintered wood throughout.

Hitler ordered his army to destroy,
all historic and cultural sites around.
The Nazis demolished most of Warsaw,
almost raising it completely to the ground.

The main station was badly bombed,
so they left earlier along the way.
As the situation's reality hit her,
Alexa immediately began to pray.

They were eighty-five miles from Łódź,
the town where they were first heading.
They began walking the ruined streets,
careful where their feet were treading.

They passed many displaced people,
walking on the roadway heading West.
Carrying a few belongings with them,
the only things they had left.

Pushing old carts and prams,
with abandoned items they'd gathered.
There were so many broken souls,
whose lives were completely shattered.

There was however, a group of Varsovians,
a mix of soldiers and Polish civilians.
Who gathered together to rebuild the city,
destroyed by the Nazi villains.

'The entire nation builds its capital,'
became the city's rallying cry.
For the love of life to come in the future,
and as a tribute to all those who had died.

They formed human volunteer lines,
passing rubble and buckets of debris.
Hard labor which Poles actually chose,
now they were physically free.

While walking on their journey,
an Allied truck passed by their way.
They hitched a ride towards Łódź,
which took the best part of the day.

Antoni arrived back in his hometown,
after so many stolen years.
He first went to find his childhood home,
where he discovered his worst fears.

114

His family no longer lived there,
new tenants had taken their place.
The young boy in him was heartbroken,
Alexa could tell by the look on his face.

Next, he walked to his grandfather's villa,
hoping to find his family there.
To the place where he'd played as a child,
when the world didn't have a care.

Antoni tried to catch his breath,
as the bombed-out villa came into view.
It was completely destroyed and lay in ruins,
as did his big inheritance dreams too.

They left that place and continued their walk,
Antoni wasn't sure where next to try.
He said he needed coffee and a smoke,
so they found a café nearby.

"Antoni, is that you?"
Asked a blonde female waitress.
In her white starched apron,
and red polka-dot dress.

"I knew you'd make it back here,
safe and alive one day."
Then she gave him a hug,
in a family kind of way.

"This is my cousin Elena,
Elena, this is Alexa my wife."
The woman seemed quite surprised,
he really had moved on with his life.

"Where is my mother?
Is she still alive?
And what about my father?
Did he survive?"

"Yes, aunty Stephanie is alive,
she'll be delighted to see you and your wife.
It has not been easy during the war,
she's had a very difficult life."

"Your father never returned home,
after his sudden arrest.
We believe he died in Stutthof,
your mother's been bereft."

She wrote down the new address,
and told him the coffees were her treat.
They said goodbye and headed off,
down the road towards his mother's street.

Arriving outside her new house,
he knocked loudly on the door.
His mother eventually answered,
and her jaw dropped to the floor.

"Hello Mamma," said Antoni,
as his mother opened the door.
"Is that you, my son?" She asked,
he didn't look like her boy anymore.

"Yes Mamma it's me, I'm home,
and this is my new wife."
She brought them into her house,
and caught up on their lost life.

She told him that his father,
never returned home since his arrest.
And that it was most likely in Stutthof,
where her husband had met his death.

Three weeks they stayed with Antoni's mom,
then Alexa could wait no more.
She longed to receive the same welcome,
when her own mother opened the door.

Stephanie gave them each a suitcase,
filled with clothes, money, and supplies.
They bought two tickets for the Lublin train,
and then said their parting goodbyes.

~ 17 ~

RETURN TO LUBLIN

After a seven-hour train journey,
they arrived in Lublin, Alexa's hometown.
It too suffered severe structural damage,
seventy percent was raised to the ground.

As she got closer to her old street,
her feet began to skip, and then run.
Her thoughts raced even faster,
the day she'd dreamt of had finally come.

She knocked on the front door,
and waited for her mother to answer.
But a middle-aged man soon appeared,
who was abrupt and a bit of a chancer.

He said he didn't know her family,
and they didn't live there anymore.
He said he didn't want any trouble,
then he firmly slammed the door.

Alexa's heart sank deeper,
and tears brimmed in her eyes.
This was not the result she'd expected,
her disappointment wore no disguise.

She went to check with her old neighbors,
Magda, Michael, and their twins.
She knocked hard on their front door,
but no one appeared to be in.

When finally, the door opened,
a woman stood on the other side.
She became suspicious of them both,
not inviting them inside.

"I'm looking for my mother and sister,
we used to live next door.
We left Asha here with the neighbors,
while we shopped at the shoe store."

"We were captured by the Nazis,
sent to a camp then torn apart.
I've not seen them in five years,
it has totally broken my heart."

"I'm sorry for what happened to you,
and the things your family went through.
But I'm glad the Germans are gone,
I'm sorry, but I can't help you."

Antoni took Alexa's hand,
and led her away from that place.
She had run out of options,
and it showed across her face.

119

She thought of her old friend Helena,
who she'd walked home that day from school.
Alexa began running to her house,
hope became her motivating fuel.

She battered on the front door,
of Helena's family home.
"Oh thank God you're alive Alexa,
I always wondered where you'd gone."

The two girls were now young women,
but hugged like they were five years old.
Helena's mother soon appeared,
happily witnessing the reunion unfold.

"Alexa, how wonderful to see you."
She flung her arms in a warm embrace.
Alexa introduced her new husband,
and their excitement levels raised.

"Do you know where my mother and Asha are?"
She couldn't wait any longer to find out.
"You better come inside my dear,
we have lots to talk about."

Helena's mother made them some coffee,
and began the difficult conversation.
"Sadly, your mother never returned home,
sorry we have no more information."

Alexa was devastated,
uncontrollably she burst into tears.
There'd be no reunion with her mother,
as she had dreamt for five long years.

"What about my dear Asha,
do you know what happened to my sister?
Since the morning we left her with Magda,
I can't tell you how much I've missed her."

"Magda looked after Asha,
when you both never came home.
They took her to live with them,
and raised her like one of their own."

Helena said she'd be right back,
returning with a package, tied with strings.
Asha had written, 'for my sister Alexa' on it,
and packed it with some personal things.

Alexa held the package close,
tracing her fingers over her sister's words.
She could almost hear Asha's voice in her head,
which seemed a little absurd.

"She lived with Magda for one year,
then your rich aunt came and took her away.
I think she lived in Rzeszów,
but we've never seen her since that day."

Tears fell from Alexa's eyes,
as she began to untie the strings.
Asha had packed their Bible,
with a note, amongst the things.

She opened the Bible and looked inside,
where she found a few family photos.
They brought back floods of fond memories,
a tsunami of waves in total.

Asha had written their aunt's address,
of where she'd been taken to live.
At least Alexa knew her sister was safe,
under the care of their wealthy relative.

The couple immediately made plans,
to collect Asha from her aunt's home.
They boarded a train bound for Rzeszów,
just as Alexa's mother would have done.

Three hours later they left the train,
and went in search of her aunt's street.
Alexa couldn't find it fast enough,
and was extremely light on her feet.

Finally, they arrived at her aunt's large house,
Alexa knocked on the front door.
It was obvious from the woman's face,
she didn't recognize her niece anymore.

Alexa began to tell her,
who she was and why she was there.
At first her Aunt Isabella seemed interested,
but soon displayed a real lack of care.

Alexa asked to see her sister,
but her aunt said she was no longer there.
"It seems my home wasn't good enough for her,
so I arranged for her to live elsewhere."

"She was always crying for you and your mother,
begging to go back to Lublin.
So, I arranged for a wealthy woman with children,
to give her a room to live in."

Alexa couldn't actually believe,
the shocking words her aunt was saying.
And the fact that it probably meant,
her sister had been domestic slaving.

"Do you have the address?
I need to find my sister.
And do you know about our mother?
I have so terribly missed her."

Isabella quickly left the room,
then returned with the woman's address.
It wasn't until asked the next question,
that the woman's guilty mouth confessed.

"No, I know nothing of your mother,
nor do I care if she's okay.
She was always little miss perfect,
I never really liked her anyway."

"How dare you talk about my mother like that,
she never really liked you either.
But at least she had manners and gave you respect,
as a good Christian and a believer."

She tossed the paper note at Alexa,
"Get out of my house," she barked.
"With daughters like you two,
it's no wonder she never came back."

"Please don't talk to my wife that way,
there's no need to be so cruel."
Antoni tried to reason with her,
but her anger had too much fuel.

"Get out, and don't come back!" She shrieked,
Alexa could feel her blood boiling.
"You would have made a good Nazi,
they were great at soul destroying."

"Or a Gestapo officer's wife."
Antoni sarcastically added.
Then they ran away from the house,
leaving the woman completely maddened.

~ 18 ~

LOOKING FOR ASHA

The couple boarded a train to Lublin,
heading back to where they started.
Alexa wasn't so much angry anymore,
as she was broken-hearted.

He asked why her aunt was so mean,
concerning Alexa's mother.
"Well, my mom always said Isabella felt,
she had married the wrong brother."

"Thank goodness she didn't marry my father,
could you imagine her as my mom?
I would have run away from home every day,
just to escape her cruel poison."

Later that October evening,
they reached the address of the woman's house.
Antoni knocked loudly on the door,
opened by a girl, as timid as a mouse.

Seeing Alexa stand in front of her,
her eyes widened in surprise.
There before her stood her big sister,
who was most definitely still alive.

"Alexa my dear sister,
is that really you?"
"Yes my darling Asha,
I've finally found you."

They cried and hugged one another,
falling into each other's arms.
"I've got you now," said Alexa,
you won't come to any more harm."

Their reunion was interrupted,
by a tall woman appearing behind the door.
"Who are you people, what's going on here?
Asha, get back to cleaning my floor."

"She doesn't work for you anymore,
I'm her sister and she's leaving with me."
"Oh no she's not, I own her,
I paid her aunt good money."

Alexa glared at the woman,
in total disbelief and disgust.
"My sister's worked her last day for you,
now move, she's coming with us."

"You'll have to wait till my husband gets home,
he always knows what to do."
"Actually, no we won't, now move!" He said,
"We are coming through."

126

It didn't take long to pack Asha's things,
she didn't actually own very much.
Alexa held her sister's hand,
they took strength from each other's touch.

They passed the woman in the hallway,
pushing their way to the front door.
She followed after them hurling abuse,
joined by her children of four.

Alexa introduced her husband,
tears again rolled down Asha's face.
Surprised and delighted all at once,
crying, "take me away from this place."

They made their way back to Helena's house,
not really having any other choice.
"Oh dear girl thank goodness you're safe,"
exclaimed Helena's mother's relieved voice.

Inside the house they settled in the lounge,
and began putting the facts together.
Asha told of her aunt's cruelty,
how she was treated like a prisoner.

Then the day she was taken to Lublin,
to slave for the wealthy woman.
Another evil and nasty creature,
who treated her as subhuman.

"My chores were never-ending,
I was locked in a room with no sun.
But no matter how dark it got,
I never forgot Psalm 91."

Alexa became emotional,
and her tears began to flow.
"I am so terribly sorry Asha.
We...We just didn't know."

"What happened to our mamma,
and where is she now?
I've thought about trying to find her,
but I don't know how."

Alexa began telling her,
what happened the day they were taken.
As she told of her nightmare journey,
vivid memories were awakened.

She spoke of her years in Germany.
as if watching on a movie screen.
Paralleling the roads they had walked,
forced to slave under Hitler's regime.

Alexa forwarded to her wedding day,
telling the women how they had met.
Asha asked to see her wedding rings,
he said, he'd not bought her proper one yet.

128

Asha reached for her small bag,
and took out a lace-up shoe.
"Since you and Mamma never came back,
I've kept these rings safe for you."

She emptied the contents of a sock,
into the center of her hand.
Then she passed them to Alexa,
who jumped to her feet to stand.

"Oh, my goodness," gasped Alexa,
how did you get Mamma's rings?"
"Don't you remember? The day you left,
these were my pretend playthings."

"My fingers are still too small at thirteen,
and I was scared they might get lost.
So I hid them in one of my old shoes,
I've protected them at all cost."

"You are married now Alexa,
you should wear them on your finger.
That way she'll forever be close,
her memory will always linger."

"I can't tell you how much this means to me,
but you obviously already know.
Thank you kindly for such a thoughtful act,
of unconditional love in flow."

Alexa placed her mother's engagement ring,
above her own wedding band.
The amethyst stone gleamed its purple light,
as she admired it on her hand.

This was the best souvenir,
Alexa could have wished for.
She wrapped her arms around Asha,
and tenderly kissed her.

"I have something special for you in return,
something which I've never lost."
Alexa reached up to her neck,
removing their grandmother's silver cross.

"I've worn it all these years,
and it's always got me through.
Now you'll wear it Asha,
so Babcia will always be with you."

"Thanks Alexa, I won't take it off,
I promise I'll wear it every day."
They both now had a piece of their past,
Alexa began to pray.

With nowhere else to go,
Helena's mother invited them to stay.
She made up extra beds,
and they slept their emotions away.

~ 19 ~

IN SEARCH OF A NEW LIFE

Morning arrived, they discussed their next move,
Antoni headed out in search of work.
He tried to register at the local town hall,
but was greeted by a suspicious clerk.

"What kind of name is Metzinger?
It sounds very German to me."
But no matter what Antoni said,
the clerk just would not believe.

"I am Polish I tell you,
I went to school in Łódź before the war."
"I don't believe you're not German,
get lost or I'll report you to the law."

Antoni had no other choice,
but to hightail it out of there.
There was no denying his German surname,
or his Aryan looks and blond hair.

He ran back to Helena's house,
to tell them the disappointing news.
They couldn't stay in Lublin now,
the three of them would have to move.

Reports in national newspapers,
told of opportunities to build a new life.
So he decided on Gryfów Śląski,
for him, Asha, and his wife.

With vacant apartments, and workers needed,
in many different professions.
They packed some food and boarded a train,
taking only their few possessions.

When they first arrived in the city,
Antoni was hired as an electrician.
The sisters got jobs in a restaurant,
clearing tables and washing dishes.

Alexa was promoted to head cook,
while Asha waited on tables.
After their first year living there,
the apartment needed a baby cradle.

Alexa was pregnant with her first child,
in August of 1946.
She gave birth to a girl named Stasha,
who thankfully wasn't sick.

The following year in September,
Alexa gave birth to her first son.
She named her baby boy Henry,
and planned to have another one.

132

In September of 1948,
her second son Richard was born.
He only lived a few short weeks,
dying suddenly in his sleep one morn.

Alexa was heartbroken,
sorrow had found her once again.
She prayed for extra endurance,
for God to help her withstand the pain.

There were bad memories attached,
from when baby Richard had died.
Antoni said they could move house,
but she couldn't forget, hard as she tried.

Since a bigger home was more expensive,
Antoni had to work extra days.
Often, he'd be gone most of the week,
Alexa missed him in many ways.

Asha met a young Polish man,
whom she fancied as her marriage mate.
Their romance quickly blossomed,
and they planned their wedding date.

During Christmas of 1948,
Alexa gave birth to her second daughter.
Having a family to raise of her own,
filled her life with joy and laughter.

In the summer of 1950,
Asha married her first love.
She prayed it'd be a good marriage,
blessed by God above.

Alexa had two more children with Antoni,
another boy, followed by another girl.
Stefan and Krystina joined the family,
her five children were Alexa's whole world.

By the time Stasha was seven,
Antoni worked more away from home.
Leaving Alexa behind with the children,
for most of the time alone.

Alexa was proud of her husband,
working hard to provide for their family.
He was promoted to senior electrician,
which raised his wage substantially.

He learned to drive a company truck,
so he now worked further away.
He said there was a job in Jelenia Góra,
which would take at least three days.

On the second day, his friend stopped by,
with information for Antoni's wife.
"I'm sorry to have to tell you this,
but your husband lives a dishonest life."

"He's been seeing a young woman,
Antoni's staying with her now.
He's told her that he'll marry her,
I think he's lost his mind somehow."

"He's so lucky to have you as his wife,
you're a beautiful woman and mother.
It's beyond me why he'd even want to look,
at any of his others."

Alexa stared in disbelief at the man,
as the blood drained from her face.
She felt sick to her stomach,
and then she felt disgrace.

She thanked the man for telling her,
even though it was devastating news.
The man obviously felt empathy for her,
as if he was walking in her shoes.

Antoni finally returned home,
after his three days of playing away.
Alexa had rehearsed repeatedly,
exactly what she wanted to say.

As he leaned over to kiss her hello,
she said, "Not with those cheating lips."
Caught off guard he tried to ignore it,
hoping it was just a silly slip.

Alexa raised her voice,
shouting out her accusations.
He tried to protest his innocence,
but was slowly losing patience.

Antoni finally lost his temper,
raising his hand to slap her face.
The children began to cry,
and ran for a hiding place.

He struck her a few more times,
then threw her down to the floor.
Uncaringly he stepped over her,
and walked out the front door.

Alexa's face ached and stung,
she had a cut on her right cheek.
She'd never seen his temper before,
nor suspected that he was a cheat.

Hours later he arrived home with flowers,
as if that would make it all okay.
He begged Alexa to forgive him,
and swore that he was truly sorry.

Alexa wore her emotional mask,
letting him think he was forgiven.
But when he left for work the next day,
he didn't know she'd made her decision.

She emptied savings from their money jar,
and bought tickets for the train.
They'd go stay with Asha in Kraków,
while deciding if she'd trust him again.

She spent five days with her sister,
then returned with her children back home.
Antoni seemed to have learned his lesson,
and said with other women, he was done.

Antoni was unable or unwilling,
to control his womanizing ways.
Alexa vowed she'd save enough money,
to leave for good with her children one day.

~ 20 ~

MAKING ENDS MEET

A few years later she made the split,
leaving with her children to a new home.
Working several jobs to provide for her family,
taking care of them on her own.

She baked bread in the early morning,
then a shift in the laundry house washing clothes.
Next, she'd cook food in the cafeteria,
then carry buckets of coal along dark roads.

She decided to try and better herself,
studying at night as a crane operator.
She passed her exams with flying colors,
a job where men were the main dominators.

As the first female crane operator,
at Gdańsk's shipbuilder's port.
Alexa was soon promoted,
as a manager of cargo transport.

The job came with its advantages,
as well as a much higher wage.
With a bigger apartment to live in,
for the first time she was able to save.

After seven years divorced from Antoni,
Alexa took a chance on love again.
She thought she'd found her life partner,
but it seems alcohol was his best friend.

After the couple were married,
she had a baby girl named Violetta.
Her five kids with Antoni were now older,
and she prayed that life would get better.

Sometimes her husband disappeared for hours,
sometimes he'd be gone for days.
One day he walked out of the door,
and never again walked back her way.

Alexa chose badly in men,
they only wanted her for her looks.
She decided to focus on her children,
and began studying art books.

She'd always had a love of painting,
her father had taught her well.
Alexa began painting flowers in oils,
and many of them she'd sell.

She maintained her special friendships,
with her three European friends.
Henrietta, Marta, and Greta,
long after the war's end.

They wrote each other letters,
and conversed over the phone.
About their children and new lives,
since they'd all returned back home.

They had gone through so much together,
and remembered the nightmare in their minds.
Their friendships had grown even stronger,
over the long passage of time.

Alexa wrote a letter to the Klausses,
a few years after the war was over.
She thanked them for freeing her,
and their cousin Edgar who drove her.

Alexa was delighted,
to receive such a warm reply.
Then they sent some generous gifts,
which took her completely by surprise.

Every few months they'd send a large parcel,
packed inside with many things.
Such as food, medicine, clothes, and shoes,
ornaments, chocolate, and rings.

Always inside of one item,
they would hide 100 Deutschmark.
She wondered if it was compensation,
some kind of retro payback.

In the spring of 1978,
the Klausses invited Alexa as their guest.
She took her eldest daughter with her,
and accepted their kind request.

Plans were soon set in motion,
Herr Klauss booked and paid for their flights.
Alexa was a little apprehensive,
but trusted their visit would be all right.

They boarded an airplane in Gdansk,
flying for the very first time.
Followed by a train ride to Bitsburg,
triggering memories in her mind.

When the train arrived at the station,
Alexa's eyes scanned the place.
She saw the blond head of Richard,
now with a much older face.

Herr Klauss's son reintroduced himself,
greeting Alexa after more than thirty years.
He was the spitting image of his father,
their resemblance was strikingly clear.

His parents still lived at the farmhouse,
Richard drove them directly there.
As he turned into the driveway,
on the back of her neck stood hair.

Frau and Herr Klauss stood outside their home,
patiently waiting to meet and greet.
They were now an elderly couple,
white-haired and unsteady on their feet.

"Alexa, it's good to see you again,
this must be your daughter Stasha."
He shook their hands and kissed both cheeks,
as was the German fashion.

"Hello Herr Klauss, good to see you both."
She addressed them as she always did.
"Please, call us by our first names,
Emile and Fredrick."

Alexa was no longer a teenager,
and these were much different times.
She decided to move on from the past,
with an open and forgiving mind.

Emile dropped with the German custom,
hugging Alexa with a warm embrace.
She had tears of joy in her eyes,
and a welcoming smile on her face.

She took them inside the farmhouse,
preparing some drinks and food to eat.
Richard carried their suitcase upstairs,
while they sat by the fire's heat.

The three Klauss kids were married,
all with children of their own.
Richard said she'd get to see them,
but it was late, and he'd a long drive home.

He said he'd return in a few days' time,
to show some sights and familiar places.
And to meet with some of the locals,
to see if she remembered their faces.

Alexa began to gather the dishes,
Emile said there was no need for that.
Alexa insisted it was not a bother,
and stacked the dirty plates flat.

Stepping through the kitchen door,
she found the scene so surreal.
Her memory sped back like a time machine,
recalling emotions she used to feel.

She sat the tray on the kitchen table,
then turned and walked back out the door.
She was no one's slave any longer,
it wasn't her job anymore.

It was after eleven o'clock,
when Emile suggested they get some sleep.
She showed them to their guest bedrooms,
which were warm, comfortable, and neat.

They gave Alexa Richard's old room,
thankfully it had been nicely redecorated.
Stasha was given Anna's old bedroom,
next door to where her mother was located.

Alexa was relieved she hadn't been placed,
in the old room where she used to sleep.
She felt it may have been too much to bare,
in her now much older feet.

The Klausses told them to feel at home,
and help themselves to what they needed.
Alexa thought of how different things were,
from how her younger self had been treated.

She went to check on Stasha,
and made sure she was all right.
Then she tucked in the blankets,
and kissed her daughter goodnight.

Again, she made the comparison,
from thirty years before.
She exited Anna's old bedroom,
and firmly closed the door.

~ 21 ~

DO YOU REMEMBER ME?

Alexa woke the next morning,
and began to recite her prayer.
She thanked her God above,
for His always being there.

Her faith in God had never faltered,
she believed without a shadow of doubt.
That He had been her constant protector,
and had kept her safe throughout.

After breakfast on the Monday,
Alexa took her daughter for a walk.
She shared some of her history,
giving them a chance to really talk.

She saw the house where Elizabeth once slaved,
and decided to knock on the door.
Wondering if her old friend's German keepers,
still lived there anymore.

The door was opened by an old woman,
who was short, with a head of white hair.
When Alexa said who she was,
the woman intensely focused her stare.

She didn't seem to remember Alexa,
until she mentioned Elizabeth's name.
"Ah yes, the slave girl from Poland,"
she said, devoid of any shame.

The woman said she lived alone,
her children had all moved away.
She invited them in for coffee,
but Alexa didn't want to stay.

She had no idea what happened to Elizabeth,
nor did she even seem to care.
Alexa made excuses, declined her invitation,
and hightailed it out of there.

Richard took them for a ride into town.
around noon on the Tuesday.
He took them to visit old neighbors for lunch,
who knew her back in the day.

They shared memories and stories,
which they recalled from the past.
The few hours spent reminiscing,
ticked by very fast.

They were given a few small parting gifts,
as forget-me-nots and souvenirs.
Stasha was amazed her mother was admired,
after the passing of so many years.

Richard said they had to leave,
checking the clock above the fireplace.
Alexa had absolutely no idea,
he'd be taking her to see Alice.

"Alexa, how wonderful to see you again,
I prayed you make it home alive.
And long after the war ended,
I hoped your soul truly thrived."

Alice was the shoemakers-wife,
who lived in Luxembourg way back then.
Where she spent her Sundays at seventeen,
with the Kleins again, and again.

She expressed her gratitude and appreciation,
as much as she possibly could.
"Thanks for your loving kindness towards me,
and making me shoes not made of wood."

They embraced in a hug once again,
their eyes expressed happiness and joy.
Richard looked on trying to understand,
he had different views as a boy.

They ate cake and drank coffee together,
while catching up on each other's lives.
Alice showed photos of her grown-up children,
with their husbands, children, and wives.

She asked Alexa to share her story,
of her treacherous journey back home.
Of what happened to her mother and sister,
on the paths which they'd walked alone.

Alexa hadn't verbalized her story,
very often over the years.
But Alice genuinely cared about her,
which her eyes expressed through tears.

She told her about the first-class ticket,
and how she made her escape from the train.
And of being locked up in the convent,
and kept as a slave again.

The bombings, the bike rides,
and the old school hall.
The truck rides, guitar player,
and her three friends, most of all.

"Compared to many others during the war,
I didn't fair so bad.
I made the best out of every situation,
and gave the very best I had."

"I was blessed by the kindness of strangers,
whom I met on the roads since I was taken.
They thankfully restored my faith in humanity,
and left my faith unshaken."

The Klausses and their cousin Edgar,
the old man with chocolate who came to her aid.
The US commander offering her stolen treasure,
and the dresses from the material she made.

Alice hung on her every word,
listening intently to Alexa talk.
She took three glasses from the cabinet,
and Richard poured them all a shot.

Alexa spoke finally about her mother,
and how she'd never seen her again.
But since she'd found her little sister,
they were inseparable, closer than best friends.

Interrupted by a knock at the door,
Alice returned with an elderly friend.
Her family wanted to meet Alexa,
before her vacation came to an end.

Alexa said she was sorry,
but her time was already planned.
The woman was persistent,
and made a prayer sign with her hands.

Finally, Alexa agreed,
since the house was fairly close by.
Alice told Alexa to visit again,
and the two of them hugged goodbye.

149

Richard parked his car outside,
of a white cottage made of stone.
On a high-backed leather chair,
was a man sitting all alone.

Richard greeted him first,
calling him Uncle Hans.
He stood up from his chair,
and shook his nephew's hand.

She figured they must be related,
from what she'd heard them say.
Hans was a tall man in his seventies,
and his hair was silver-gray.

"Hello Alexa, do you remember me?"
Hans said, staring into her blue eyes.
"I'm sorry Sir, but I'm afraid I do not."
He didn't seem very surprised.

"It was me who paid your ticket on the train,
when you were yelled at by the conductor."
Stunned by the unexpected revelation,
the reality of the situation struck her.

"Yes, the train, I remember you now."
But Alexa couldn't make sense of it.
Hans gave her a gentle hug, then said,
"I realize how intense this is."

150

"Thank you ever so kindly,
I'm very grateful you were there."
"That's the way my cousin and I planned it,
so you'd be under my watchful care."

"Fredrick couldn't tell you our plan,
in case you gave the game away.
There were many soldiers on the train,
who'd have shot you for being Polish that day."

Alexa thanked him repeatedly,
as the penny finally dropped, and she got it.
This was by far the greatest gesture of kindness,
where the giver received no profit.

He asked what happened at the convent,
after her long trek through the woods.
Alexa said the nuns were mean to her,
that the whole experience wasn't good.

"She was always my least favorite cousin,
it was Fredrick's idea to add her to our plans.
At least the Allied forces finished her off,
when bombers took her life in their hands."

Han's wife brought coffee to the table,
and a crystal decanter of brandy.
Richard poured them all a small glass,
then to each, one was handed.

"Here's to surviving!" Said Hans,
raising his glass to make the toast.
Everyone replied, "To surviving."
Hans seemed to need his drink the most.

He placed his empty glass on the table,
said, "Wait here!" Then disappeared.
He returned carrying an old suitcase,
which looked like it had seen better years.

"This is for you," said Hans,
a souvenir from our train ride long ago.
It's for you and your family now,
you can use it to travel wherever you go."

Reluctantly, Alexa accepted the gift,
realizing Hans would be hurt if she said no.
Richard said it was getting late,
and they really had to go.

"I'll never forget what you did for me Hans,
all those years ago."
"I'm happy I could help in some small way,
to get you back home."

She hugged Hans goodbye,
for the last time they'd ever meet.
Richard placed the suitcase in the car,
with Stasha, waving from the back seat.

~ 22 ~

A LIFE LIVED WELL

"That was an unexpected surprise,"
still trying to work it all out in her head.
"Yes, we knew you wouldn't expect it,
so we kept it our little secret instead."

"I don't recall Hans living,
in the town when I was here."
"That's because he didn't."
He answered back, short and clear.

"When did he move here,
and what was his job?"
Richard took a few moments,
then began speaking after a pause.

"British soldiers arrived at our farmhouse,
my father was arrested and taken away.
All because he was an officer,
following the orders, he was forced to obey."

"All he did was protect Hitler's artwork,
collected for his super museum.
He was never in any of those camps,
he said he'd never even seen them."

153

"Uncle Hans was arrested in Berlin,
so Aunt Danka came to live here.
They were both tried at Nuremberg,
and imprisoned for several years."

"Don't tell my parents I've told you,
they don't like it being talked about.
It wasn't easy for my father,
there was much my family did without."

Alexa could no longer hold back her words,
and released what she'd never said.
"Well, it wasn't easy for me either Richard,"
his face began to turn red.

"Rounded up and separated,
from my mother at age thirteen.
Then forced to slave for your family,
for five years I cooked and cleaned."

"I didn't mean to be insensitive,
forgive me, I didn't think."
"It's okay, apology accepted."
Alexa said, with a forgiving wink.

Richard had enough of conversation,
he turned the knob on the car's radio.
A Billie Holiday song was playing,
which young Stasha seemed to know.

"God bless the child...,
whose got his own..."
Oblivious to their conversation,
she hummed the chorus alone.

Their stay with the Klausses went well,
but they never talked about the shame.
Of Germans taking European children,
to slave for their own selfish gain.

When she arrived back home to Poland,
she unpacked the suitcase given by Hans.
It came in useful for carrying the gifts,
they'd received while in German land.

Alexa locked the old black suitcase,
placing it on top of the wardrobe in her room.
It became one of her treasured possessions,
a reminder of how close she came to doom.

Alexa held no malice,
she wasn't consumed by hate.
She never needed an apology,
from the Klausses served on a plate.

'The truth lies in the behavior,
words are easy,' Alexa learned to trust.
But through their kind actions towards her,
'Sorry' never needed to be discussed.

155

The Klausses continued sending parcels,
as did their children for years to come.
Alexa's telephone always rang,
from family, friends, and old war chums.

Alexa's five children with Antoni,
all had one daughter, each born a year apart.
Four of them were born in Poland,
except for Stefan's daughter, her sweetheart.

Stefan married a young Scottish woman,
visiting her father's family in Słupsk.
Cousins introduced their handsome friend,
and from that day Rebecca was hooked.

Alexa was absolutely delighted,
her son was actually settling down.
She gave them her amethyst engagement ring,
before he moved to her Scottish town.

Stefan was like his father in many ways,
they shared the same handsome good looks.
But he followed in his father's footsteps,
with women's hearts, they were crooks.

Rebecca gave birth to their only daughter,
a brown-haired girl they named Rochelle.
The proud new mother was approached in the street,
by a neighbor with a secret to tell.

Stefan had been having an affair,
with the wife of a local art teacher.
He thought he'd get away with his deceit,
but the informant was the local shopkeeper.

Rebecca was devastated,
and quickly filed for divorce.
However, her relationship with Alexa,
grew much stronger in due course.

Rochelle first met Alexa in Poland,
when she was only two years of age.
For the grandmother, it was love at first sight,
and when Rochelle began learning her ways.

Rebecca became like a daughter to Alexa,
their relationship was a very special one.
But never could she answer her burning question,
"Where is Stefan, my son?"

Every other summer during school vacation,
Rebecca would visit Alexa with Rochelle.
The family never spoke English,
but as a child, she learned to speak Polish well.

When she was only seven years of age,
Alexa began teaching her how to paint.
Showing how to mix colors in oils,
and blend the brushstrokes they'd create.

"Practice and perseverance,"
that's what Alexa said it took.
So Rochelle kept on practicing,
and eventually became rather good.

The artistic gene passed to Alexa's kids,
except for Stefan, whom it seemed to skip.
Rochelle was the only granddaughter out of five,
who had her Babcia's artistic gift.

After visiting Auschwitz with her mother one year,
when Rochelle was thirteen years of age.
She pencil sketched the liberated children,
expressing her emotions on a blank page.

The drawing was of two young Jewish girls,
holding up their small, tattooed arms.
The image would haunt Rochelle for years,
she prayed they'd found peace and calm.

Alexa peered over her shoulder that day,
and was visibly moved by Rochelle's drawing.
Perhaps it was the thought of her own little sister,
that made Alexa's tears start falling.

Rochelle assumed her grandmother,
was tearing up due to immense pride.
Not knowing at that time,
the childhood scars she carried inside.

Alexa kissed her granddaughter's forehead,
then turned and walked out the door.
The teenager continued sketching,
creating the emotion, she was hoping for.

The experience of visiting Auschwitz,
was a powerful lesson for Rochelle.
A testimony to the worst of humanity,
and those forced to exist, or die in hell.

She learned that hate was a poison,
which can spread like a pandemic.
As if infecting a person's bloodstream,
out of control, it becomes systemic.

~ 23 ~

9/11 LEAVING NY

When Rochelle was thirteen years of age,
her mother gave her the amethyst ring.
The rectangular stone held by four golden claws,
became one of her most treasured things.

Since it had once belonged to Sophia,
and to both Alexa and her own mother.
It had a special sentimental value,
more than almost any other.

And because Asha had guarded it,
keeping it safely hidden for five years.
It added an extra priceless value,
making it especially dear.

When Rochelle was eighteen years old,
she worked for a Glasgow newspaper.
She was offered a position abroad,
in New York's city of skyscrapers.

She took the job and moved to the States,
where she lived for twelve long years.
Life was good in America,
until the world witnessed its worst fears.

Alexa never wanted her granddaughter,
to remain living in New York.
She always made that clear,
when Rochelle called long distance to talk.

Tuesday morning of September eleventh,
began with a beautiful clear blue sky.
Until four hijacked airplanes,
caused so many innocent people to die.

The first plane veered off-course,
flying towards lower Manhattan.
It headed for the World Trade Centre,
the twin towers it aimed to flatten.

People in downtown New York City,
witnessed the nightmare with their own eyes.
As hijacking terrorists flew above,
then disappeared from the cloudless skies.

American Airlines Flight 11,
crashed into the North Tower.
Causing chaos in the financial district,
attempting to weaken America's power.

The airplane hit its target,
crashing into the ninety-third floor.
The world-famous New York landmark,
would never be the same anymore.

The aircraft exploded on impact,
releasing a huge ball of fire at the top.
Blowing windows and debris into the air,
from the seventeen-hundred-foot drop.

The horrific events were broadcast live,
on televisions across the world.
Then a second American Airlines plane,
into the South Tower was hurled.

United Flight 175 flew into the structure,
crashing above the 77th floor.
The once tall pillars of power and strength,
were not safe to be in anymore.

Panic filled New Yorkers,
gazing up at the hellish sight.
Realizing the terrifying nightmare,
facing all those still trapped inside.

Police officers and fire engines,
arrived immediately at the scene.
In a desperate attempt to save lives,
by any possible means.

One hour and forty-two minutes later,
both towers collapsed and fell to the ground.
A thick toxic cloud of debris filled the air,
while alarms whistled warning sounds.

American Airlines Flight 77,
was the third flying missile that day.
It flew into the west side of the Pentagon,
confirming pure evil was at play.

United Flight 93 diverted from its path,
flying towards Washington DC.
But passengers onboard with cell phones,
were already alerted to live scenes on TV.

Passengers attempted to regain control,
by storming the highjacked flight deck.
Over the scorched Pennsylvanian ground,
lay the disintegrated wreck.

There were almost 3,000 killed that day,
when so many innocent lives were destroyed.
But for the heartbroken souls left behind to grieve,
there was a deep unfillable void.

The footprints of the twin towers,
became 'The Pit' at Ground Zero.
Where emergency crews and local volunteers,
became New York City Heroes.

They formed human lines removing rubble,
in the search and rescue phase.
Working around the clock to find survivors,
before entering the recovery stage.

The world was forever changed that day,
when Al-Qaeda unleashed its attacks fueled by hate
They proudly gave thanks to their God,
chanting repeatedly 'Allah is great.'

America's political powers went to war,
and were determined to get their revenge.
They claimed weapons of mass destruction existed,
and must be brought to their end.

Sons and daughters from America's Allies,
waged war and fought against Iraq.
Sadly, countless more lives were lost,
and many soldiers never came back.

Living in New York that day,
Rochelle was rocked to her very core.
She had never witnessed such hatred,
firsthand in her life, before.

Rochelle decided to leave New York,
realizing just how short life could be.
She weighed up her priorities,
since there were no life guarantees.

She returned to live in Scotland,
and to all that she once knew.
Nothing much had changed in twelve years,
the same people did what they always do.

She booked a flight to Kraków,
for a long overdue visit with her grandmother.
Alexa had always been her number one,
whom she only knew, thanks to her own mother.

Alexa was delighted,
her 'Rachella' was coming to visit at last.
She wrote the date on her calendar,
and marked off each day as it passed.

Their reunion was a beautiful one,
they hugged in a tender embrace.
Alexa stroked her granddaughter's hair,
and kissed her gently on her face.

Alexa already prepared a fresh batch,
of Ruskie pierogis for Rochelle.
And always had them ready to serve,
when she first rang the doorbell.

They spent hours on end, chatting away,
in catch-up conversations.
About family, life, God,
and all of His marvelous creations.

Alexa began to recite her prayer,
the familiar words of Psalm 91.
She still said it faithfully morning and night,
just as she had always done.

She said she'd learned it as a child,
in rhyme form when she was at school.
Written by the poet Jan Kochanowski,
in life it'd been her survival tool.

Rochelle shared some stories and photos,
from her twelve years living in New York.
Alexa hung on her every word,
listening to her granddaughter talk.

"I wish you'd seen Manhattan's skyline,
from the Brooklyn Bridge's view.
And Central Park in springtime,
when everything's fresh and new."

Alexa asked if she'd been to Brooklyn,
wanting to know what it was like there.
"Yes, that's where I bought your BKNY shirt,
the one I mailed for you to wear."

Alexa recalled it fondly,
and said she'd kept it as good as new.
"I remember you had a thing for Brooklyn,
what was the connection with you?"

Alexa paused for a few moments,
then a smile began to show.
"His name was Mark Austin,
I could have married him you know?"

166

Rochelle was surprised by what she heard,
and wanted to know more.
She asked her gran to tell her story,
of what happened during the war.

Alexa told her it would take some time,
and asked her to make some fresh tea.
She began to tell her history,
once they were both sitting comfortably.

~ 24 ~

HISTORY REVEALED

Life could have been so much different,
if I'd chosen Mark from Brooklyn instead.
He was a handsome American soldier,
I wonder if he's still alive, or dead?"

"But if I didn't marry Antoni,
I wouldn't have the beautiful family I do.
My wonderful children and granddaughters,
and my princess and balsam, you."

"Thank goodness you did marry Antoni,
and that you became his wife.
You're my sunshine, my diamond, my heart,
I couldn't live without you in my life."

Rochelle directed Alexa's attention,
to the amethyst ring on her finger.
Her grandmother looked at it fondly,
as distant memories lingered.

"It belonged to my mother originally,"
then she held it close to her heart.
"And since my mother gifted it to me," Rochelle said,
"This ring and I, have never been apart."

Alexa had never learned the truth,
about her mother's demise.
There was no official date of death,
nor a grave to lay flowers beside.

Red Cross records reported,
she'd been hospitalized due to a severe beating.
But most patients were killed near war's end,
by German soldiers retreating.

"My poor mamma," wept Alexa,
as her eyes released its tears.
The pain from the past was still raw,
after the passing of so many years.

Alexa started from the beginning,
when out with her mother buying new shoes.
She spoke of being rounded up in Lublin,
despite the fact they weren't Jews.

She told of the horrific nightmare,
she and her mother were forced to endure.
How they were violently torn apart,
unaware of their bleak future.

Alexa said it was her faith in God,
which she relied on to get her through.
Reciting Psalm 91 as her source of strength,
she believed His promises would come true.

"I never felt completely alone,
God was always by my side.
No matter how dark times got for me,
I grasped His right hand as my guide."

"We were all created in God's image,
and made from His perfect love.
He gave all mankind free will,
and the choice to serve God above."

"I do not hold man's evil against the true God,
for evil does not exist in Him.
Hate is a poison from a wicked source,
and God will never let the Devil win."

"Always choose love over hate in life,
and your record with God will be clean.
There is a rich reward for doing what's right,
and it's for that hope that I dream."

"Thy kingdom come, thy will be done,
on earth as it is in heaven.
That's what His son told us to pray for,
and what the meek shall be given."

"They shall inherit the earth,
and live forever upon it.
With an abundance of peace,
and the perfect health to enjoy it."

Alexa continued telling her story,
of when she returned to see the Klausses.
And being introduced to Hans their cousin,
while visiting German families' houses.

Rochelle was amazed to hear it was him,
who had paid Alexa's ticket on the train.
And that he'd given the gift of a suitcase,
to use when she travelled again.

"Babcia, your life's been incredible,
you should write it all down in a book.
I bet it would become a bestseller,
a real page-turner with a great hook."

"My history plays over in my mind,
like a reel of old war movie takes.
But I'm an old woman now,
look how my hand shakes."

"You should write it my darling,
if it's something you'd want to do.
So the world knows about what happened,
to both Polish Gentile and Jew."

Alexa had never used the suitcase,
after she arrived back home from the trip.
She kept it locked on top of her wardrobe,
its dimensions were just the right fit.

Rochelle asked if she could lift it down,
to take a closer look at the case.
Alexa said it was okay with her,
with a curious look on her face.

"You'll need the keys to open it,
they're in a heart shaped box in that drawer.
It's been so long since it's been opened,
I almost forgot what those keys were for."

Next to the large wardrobe,
Rochelle placed a wooden chair.
Reaching up for the old black suitcase,
she lifted it down with care.

Its surface was covered in a film of dust,
and cobwebs clung to its sides.
It seemed deceptively heavy,
for a case with nothing inside.

She rested it on the table,
and inserted the two small keys.
She turned them anti-clockwise,
and both sprung open with ease.

She lifted up the lid,
but there was nothing contained inside.
She wondered if there were any secrets,
someone had chosen to hide.

The interior dimensions seemed smaller,
than Rochelle thought they ought to be.
She knocked on the base of the suitcase,
but it didn't sound empty.

She undid the velvet lining,
and pulled it open wide.
Beneath was a piece of hardwood,
screwed in place to the bottom side.

Using a knife she released the screws,
and carefully lifted it out.
It didn't look like anything special,
until she flipped it about.

As she went to put it back in place,
she discovered a folded piece of paper.
An old note written by hand,
which someone obviously meant for later.

She passed the note to her grandmother,
who read out what it said.
She repeated it three times,
trying to make sense of it in her head.

'This is for you Alexa,
from the Klauss family, sorry.'
It was an undiscovered apology,
from a dark chapter in her history.

Rochelle examined the suitcase again,
for anything left hidden inside.
But there was nothing she could find,
as the Klausses note had implied.

She lifted the piece of hardwood,
to place it back inside.
But as she tilted it towards her,
Alexa's eyes opened wide.

There was a piece of old canvas,
attached to the back.
She loosened the four corners,
until the canvas became slack.

She held it by its edges,
then flipped it round the other way.
Revealing a bright oil painting of an artist,
walking by fields on a hot summer's day.

Dressed in casual blue clothing,
carrying art supplies in his right hand.
Holding a canvas under his left arm,
while baking in the sun's warm balm.

"I can't believe you've discovered this,
how could it have been here all this time?"
Alexa couldn't believe her eyes,
nor register it in her mind.

Examining it closely,
Rochelle said "Could it really be?
Does it remind you of any artist,
from back in history?"

She powered up her laptop,
and typed some words in the search.
'Second world war stolen paintings'
it wouldn't take much research.

There displayed on her computer screen,
was the exact same painting from the case.
They both couldn't believe their eyes,
or disguise the shock on their face.

On the list of stolen paintings,
Vincent van Gogh appeared at number two.
'Painter on his way to work'
now filled the full screen of her view.

"If this is the real missing masterpiece,"
can you imagine what it's worth?"
Not to mention the media frenzy,
when the world discovers what we've unearthed."

Alexa looked at the painting then said,
"I can't keep it because it isn't mine.
I now know it was stolen by the Nazis,
during Hitler's war back in thirty-nine."

"Darling, can you help me find out,
to whom it rightly belongs?
Maybe we can return it to their family,
rectifying a terrible wrong."

Rochelle agreed to help find a way,
to return it to its rightful owners.
But for a while they'd get to enjoy it,
as its unexpected loaners.

Alexa asked her to make some Earl Grey tea,
and bring the Belgian chocolates through.
"He's my most favorite artist you know,
and the reason I paint sunflowers too."

Rochelle poured two shots of Spirytus,
to toast the artist's missing piece.
"Here's to Vincent," Rochelle said,
raising her glass to the masterpiece.

Alexa lifted her glass once more,
toasting the painting they'd just exhumed.
"Here's to you, me, and Vincent.
Three artists in the one room."

The end.

ENDNOTES

Acknowledgments

First of all, my thanks go to Alexa, my fabulous grandmother, my sunshine, my diamond, my heart. My Babcia was such a beautiful soul, inside and out, and I treasure my many precious memories and conversations shared with her, as well as her unconditional love. Second, I thank my wonderful mother, for making sure I had such a special relationship with Alexa, even though she was divorced from my father, Alexa's son. Despite the distance from Scotland to Poland, my mom took me to visit my Polish family as a child during summer vacations. For that, and her unwavering love and support, I'm forever grateful. I love you mum, and I dedicate this book to you. Xo

To everyone who has encouraged my re-telling of Alexa's story, and appreciate the wonderful woman she was, I'm truly grateful. Thank you for reading, reviewing & recommending *IN ALEXA'S SHOES* and for taking my grandmother into your hearts. The many emails from random readers around the world have warmed my heart beyond measure.

Dorothy, thanks for your unwavering friendship, loyalty & support over the last 33 years. We are family… You make my world a better place to live. To our CT & NY tribe, I love all of your vibrant vibes, thanks for loving Alexa & me. Thank you, Justine my Polish/American friend, for your encouragement and enthusiasm, since day one of my writing journey.

Wilma & Nico, thank you for always promoting *IN ALEXA'S SHOES*, and for your loyal friendship and love. To Nicola, Christine, Marie & Millie, some friendships last a lifetime, thank you for being a special part of mine for so long, and for loving Alexa. May good health and happiness surround you all.

My gratitude and thanks go to Mary Turner Thomson, for editing and assistance in bringing this version of Alexa's story to publication.

To all my fabulous friends, fans, and readers on social media around the globe, thank you kindly for your outstanding support and for sharing the love. It's thanks to y'all, that Alexa remains a #1 Bestseller on Amazon USA daily. If you enjoyed this book of rhyme, please continue to leave 5-star reviews online for Alexa & me, they make a huge difference in an author's world.

The long-awaited sequel to *IN ALEXA'S SHOES* has now been penned, I hope to publish it in 2023. The new title is **ALEXA'S HEART**. For the many readers wanting to know what happened to the Van Gogh, after you read the sequel, you will know. Book #2 picks up where book #1 ends. Check my website for publication details, my friends.

Love is the answer. Xo

RochelleAlexandra.com

PHOTOGRAPHS

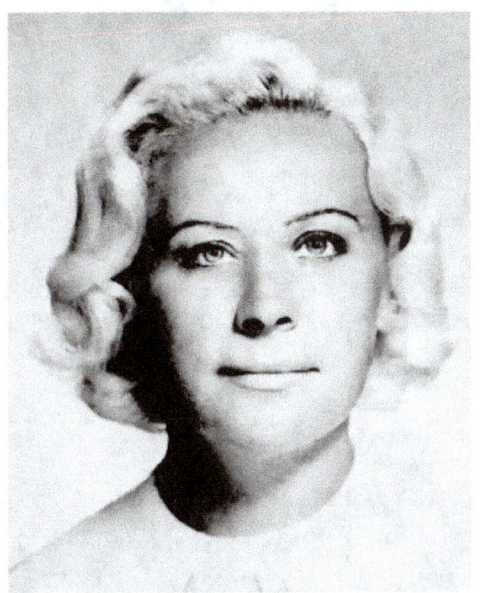

ALEXA, Gdansk, Poland, 1965

Alexa & Antoni Mourmelon,
France, 1945

Antoni's Grandfather with his family,
his father Fritz, is the one on the left.

Asha, Rochelle & Alexa. Kraków, Poland, 1993

| Asha & Alexa Kraków, Poland, 1991 | Alexa, Kraków, Poland, 2002 | Alexa & Asha, Kraków, Poland, 1992 |

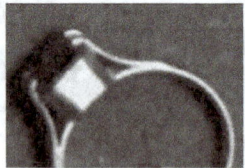

Alexa's amethyst engagement ring, stolen in Glasgow, Scotland, by convicted murderer Jason Evans Graham, January 2012. There is a reward for the rings return.

Rochelle, 1975

Alexa, Słupsk, Poland, 2008

Rochelle & Alexa, Kraków,
Poland, 1987

Alexa & Rochelle,
Kraków, Poland, 1975

Alexa & Rochelle,
Słupsk, Poland, 2008

Rochelle & Alexa,
Kraków, Poland, 1986

'Sunflower' Painting by Alexa,
Ustka, Poland, 1980s

Rochelle at Van Gogh Live,
Edinburgh, Scotland, 2022

'Painter on his way to work' by Vincent van Gogh, France, 1888

Website
RochelleAlexandra.com

Buy a copy of
IN ALEXA'S SHOES

The long-awaited sequel to *IN ALEXA'S SHOES*
has now been penned.

ALEXA'S HEART
- Scars of Love, War & Deceit –

For information and updates on when the new novel will be
published, later in 2023, please visit my website.

RochelleAlexandra.com
Email: RochelleAlexandra@outlook.com

PSALM 91

The reference to Psalm 91 used throughout this book of rhyme, *WALKING IN ALEXA'S SHOES*, refers to a direct quote from the renowned 16th Century Polish poet, Jan Kochanowski.

In the original novel *IN ALEXA'S SHOES*, I've used a mix of various Biblical verses in the chapter combined and have written the passage out into one long verse in chapter 1. It should be noted that my version, is a combination of text from several Biblical versions sighting Psalm 91; including The King James, The New World Translation, and The American Standard Version, for easier understanding and comprehension throughout the original story.

The 91st Psalm Alexa recites and refers to throughout both works, is from an old Polish Church song taken from the 16th Century Polish poet, Jan Kochanowski, once widely learned by young Polish children in school. The English translation of this version is written below. It is the version which Alexa, up until the age of 92, continued to recite off by heart as her daily prayer.

16th Century Polish poet, Jan Kochanowski, Poem based on Psalm 91. (Translated)

Who will give himself up to His Lord,
And trust in Him sincerely from the bottom of his heart.
Can say boldly: I have protection in God,
No scary awe will ever come at me.
He sets you free from the traps.
And saves you from infected air,
In the shadow of His wings, He'll keep you forever,
Underneath His feathers you will lie safely.
His stable shield and a solid buckler,

Standing behind them, neither about a nightmare,
About a fright nor about any arrows don't you care,
Which we are lavished in on the way in broad light.
A thousand heads turn to You from here,
The imminent sword will not reach You,
And You, amazed by what Your eyes saw,
You will live to see the unavoidable revenge over the sinners.
If you say to the Lord, You are my hope,
If the Highest God is your escape,
No bad experience will ever come your way,
And no damage will happen to your home.
He made His angels watch over you,
Wherever you step, they will care about you,
Will carry you in their arms, so while you're walking,
No sharp stone can hurt your feet.
You will tread on impatient,
Venomous snakes and slow worms safely.
You will mount the vicious lion without fear.
And you will ride a giant dragon.
Hear the Lord speak: "Anyone who loves Me,
And honestly walks along with Me,
Then I will love him back in all his trouble.
And I won't forget and will indeed help him.
His voice won't be condemned in Me,
I will protect him in the fight,
Let him be sure of happiness and good heartedness,
And of long lifetime and of My thoughtfulness."

ENDORSEMENTS & REVIEWS FOR IN ALEXA'S SHOES

'In Alexa's Shoes is a profoundly moving, immense story of loss, courage and faith which explores the depths of the human heart. The author's connection to Alexa is evident, beautifully captured and preserved by a loving granddaughter. It will make you cry tears of outrage and wonder leaving you inspired by the courage of a young girl. It is an extraordinary story ... everyone should read it ... I recommend it unreservedly.'
- Heather Morris, New York Times bestselling author.

'In Alexa's Shoes is a chilling, remarkable story that evoked many emotions within me. Tales that were so vivid, you could picture them as clear as a movie on a big screen. In Alexa's Shoes should be read by all and it should be immortalized as a movie.' *- kraftireader.*

'What a fantastic story that could not come at a more critical time! That becomes a vital lesson in human nature and the resilience of faith. Alexa's story is a parable for the ages from which many people can learn.' *- firefliesandfreekicks.*

'I for one think that this is a revelation. A true story with a human element that you cannot fail to be moved by. Every story of those who suffered needs to be told.' *- lipsquidbookblog.*

'Brilliantly written. A timely read. In fact, this book should be required reading for modern history students.' *- gingerbookgeek.*

★ ★ ★ ★ ★

TRAGEDY & BEAUTY THREADED TOGETHER

★ ★ ★ ★ ★

BRILLIANT STORY OF SURVIVAL

★ ★ ★ ★ ★

POWERFUL & PROFOUND

★ ★ ★ ★ ★

TRULY INSPIRING

★ ★ ★ ★ ★

FAITH BUILDING

★ ★ ★ ★ ★

BEAUTIFUL

★ ★ ★ ★ ★

~AMAZON~

ABOUT THE AUTHOR

Rochelle Alexandra was born in Glasgow, Scotland, and matured in New York, in the 1990s. As well as having a passion for writing award winning poetry and gripping stories, Rochelle is also a talented artist and photographer. She expresses her inherited artistic genes from Alexa in her creations of paintings, portraits, murals & commissions.

After hearing Alexa's WWII survival story, Rochelle promised her grandmother she'd reimagine & write her incredible life story into a novel, and finally did. This is the Rhyme version of *IN ALEXA'S SHOES*, the author's award-winning, #1 International bestselling, debut novel, based on Alexa's life story.

Rochelle's pencil sketch of two liberated children from
Auschwitz, Kraków, Poland, 1985. Second sketch, 2022.

I always wondered what happened to the two young Jewish girls in my 1983 pencil sketch, once they were liberated from Auschwitz. After drawing the updated sketch in 2022, I now know. Incredibly, I got to meet the young girl on the left, a true survivor. You can learn more about my meeting with Tova Friedman, in New York on 9/11, 2022 on my website.

Hate is a poison. Love is the answer!
We must never forget!

www.ingramcontent.com/pod-product-compliance
Lightning Source LLC
Chambersburg PA
CBHW060327260626
47160CB00007B/2714